THE WALLS COME TUMBLING DOWN

By Lou Mindar

Driftless House Publishing

Published in the United States by Driftless House Publishing.

Grateful acknowledgment is made for use of previously published material: BMG Platinum Songs o/b/o BMG 10 Music Limited and BMG Rights Management: Excerpt from "Everybody Wants to Rule the World," words and music by Christopher Hughes, Roland Orzabal, and Ian Stanley, copyright © 1985 by BMG Platinum Songs. All rights administered by BMG Rights Management

Library of Congress Cataloging-in-Publication Data
Mindar, Lou (1959 -)
The Walls Come Tumbling Down / Lou Mindar. – First Edition.
[Novel]
Pages cm
ISBN 978-0-9972488-4-5 (paperback)

Printed in the United States

DriftlessHouse.com

For my sister Cindy and her family,
And as always,
For Shelby and Louis

*"There's a room where the light won't find you,
holding hands while the walls come tumbling down."*

–Tears for Fears ("Everybody Wants to Rule the World")

CHAPTER 1

Eric Simms stood at the edge of pit lane, the roar of the 750 horse-power IndyCar engines slicing through the humid air like a war cry. The crowd was electric, a pulsing wave of voices rising and falling with each pass of the cars on the historic oval of the Indianapolis Motor Speedway. It was a symphony of chaos, a visceral jolt straight to his veins, setting his pulse racing even before he climbed into the cockpit.

He took a deep breath, inhaling the heavy scent of burning rubber and high-octane fuel, then donned his helmet, specially painted for the big race. The intricate design was a tribute to Alex Zanardi, his driving hero. Zanardi's iconic pineapple—a symbol of luck and resilience—was painted on the back of the helmet, its bright yellow and green hues sparkling in the bright sunlight.

Eric slid into the cockpit of his Dallara single-seater race car, the air stagnant in the small space around him. He adjusted his gloves, feeling the smooth, tight fabric against his palms. His hands tightened around the formula-style steering wheel, then he loosened his grip and began drumming his fingers on the wheel as he waited his turn to qualify for the biggest race of the year. The Indianapolis 500—the crown jewel of motorsport.

Qualifying for the Indy 500 was unlike any other race in the world. Four laps around the two-and-a-half mile track, the fastest four-lap average wins the pole for the Memorial Day classic.

The week leading up to qualifying had unfolded perfectly, every moment of practice pushing him closer toward his goal. Throughout the sessions, the car had felt dialed in—fast on the straights and responsive in the turns. Eric had been among the fastest drivers each practice session, and on Fast Friday, when the turbo boost was cranked up on the engines, he had been the fastest of them all.

Once he reached the head of the qualifying line, the IndyCar official motioned for him to head onto the empty track. The engine's growl filled the air as Eric's fingers gripped the wheel, tightening ever so slightly. Time to shine.

The rear wheels spun as he launched out of pit lane, the engine's roar reverberating through the chassis. For the warmup laps, he was cautious, easing into the throttle. Too much speed now could burn off his tires. Instead, he took it slow, gently warming the engine, mindful not to overstrain his Firestones. Every detail mattered.

"Give me four good, clean laps," the voice over his radio crackled, calm and steady. Mike Bedrosian, his strategist, had been the voice in his ear for every twist and turn since he'd joined Catalyst Racing. His three IndyCar victories over the past two seasons had all been achieved with Mike's guidance.

Eric's heart pounded in his ears, his pulse syncing with the rhythm of the roaring engines. Indianapolis qualifying was a different beast. It was flat-out, no holds barred, the car constantly on the edge of disaster. One mistake—a lapse in concentration, a gust of wind—could send him hurtling into the wall. But having Mike's voice, familiar and reassuring, in his ear calmed him.

He made his way around the famous track to the start-finish line, feeling the car respond like a living, breathing entity. The slight chatter of the tires, the whisper of the wind, every sensation was amplified inside the bubble of the car. He would take it easy through turns one and two, letting the car breathe, and then he would push it hard down the back stretch. By the time he crossed the start-finish line again, he needed to be going as fast as his car and the conditions would allow.

The car responded to his touch, his foot pressing firmly down on the throttle, the engine at full song. He shifted through the gears, turning the wheel ever so slightly to guide the car through turn three. The balance was there; predictable, steady, like an old dancing partner. Eric thought about the importance of the next four laps. It was a long race and anything could happen, but his odds of doing well—maybe even winning—would be improved with a good starting position. But he could worry about that later. Now, he needed to concentrate on hitting his marks.

Mike's voice crackled over the radio. "Use your tools. Stay smooth. Next lap is green."

Eric exhaled slowly, the weight of the moment settling into his bones. This was it.

"Eric Simms approaches the green flag to start lap one of four," announcer Will Buxton said in his distinct English-accent.

"Simms has been among the fastest drivers all month," race analyst James Hinchcliffe added. "He showed signs of being fast in his previous Indy 500 starts, but this year, in this car, might be his best chance yet to win the biggest race of the year."

The television cut to Eric as he navigated turns one and two with precision, the car gliding through the corners.

"Let's see what his trap speed is heading into turn three." Hinchcliffe's voice was full of expectation. "Oh, 241 miles per hour. That's the fastest trap speed we've seen yet."

Eric soared through turn four, his focus absolute, as the car's tires kissed the asphalt, the roar of the engine a high-pitched, vibrating growl beneath him.

"Simms' first lap is…" Buxton paused, his voice filled with suspense. "Wow! 234.525 miles per hour. That's the fastest first lap we've had thus far in qualifying."

"And he's not slowing down," Hinchcliffe said. "He's fast into turn one and through the short chute to turn two." The camera followed Eric's progress through turn two, and then down the backstretch. "It will be interesting to see how fast he is into turn three this lap."

Buxton's voice came alive with excitement. "He touched 241 miles per hour again."

"Simms still looks solid coming through turn four," Hinchcliffe said. "His hands have been quiet on the steering wheel, indicating his car is doing exactly what he's asking of it."

"Eric Simms crosses the line to complete lap two with a speed of…" Buxton hesitated. "…234.134 miles per hour."

"That's not much of a fall off at all," Hinchcliffe said. "This is going to be a monster qualifying run for Simms, assuming he can hang on to it for two more laps."

Mike's voice over the radio played on the television broadcast, the urgency of the moment betrayed by his calm tone. "Lap three. Don't forget your tools."

"When Simms' strategist, Mike Bedrosian, tells Eric to use his tools, he's talking about the weight jacker and the anti-roll bar," Hinchcliffe explained. "The driver can use those tools—moving the weight jacker left or right—and the anti-roll bar—making the front suspension softer or stiffer—to help him go through the turns."

"In turn three, we're beginning to see some fall off from Simms," Buxton noted. "His top speed this lap in turn three was 239 miles per hour."

"As the tires wear, we expect to see a little fall off each lap," Hinchcliffe said.

"Lap three for Simms is…233.698 miles per hour."

"Still, very impressive," Hinchcliffe said. "One lap to go."

"Simms, the former F1 reserve, has been among the top IndyCar drivers since returning to the United States and joining the series," Buxton said. "We could be seeing his best qualifying effort here at Indianapolis in just one more lap."

"He's through turns one and two cleanly," Hinchcliffe noted. "Let's see how his trap speed compares to previous laps."

There was a pause, then Buxton chimed in. "Another 239 miles per hour. He's still…"

"Whoa!" Hinchcliffe exclaimed. "A big wiggle from Simms heading into turn four… Oh no!"

Eric entered turn three and the car initially responded to his input, but then suddenly—too suddenly—the rear of the car stepped out. Eric steered into the slide, the tires screaming in protest.

For a split second, he thought he could catch the slide and still make the turn. But as he closed in on turn four, the car swapped ends, spinning beyond his control, the rear of the car heading toward the wall. The steering wheel went slack. His vision blurred as the track flew past him. He took his hands off the steering wheel and held his arms tight against his body, preparing for the inevitable.

The television broadcast showed Eric's car strike the turn four wall with a sickening crunch, then launch into the air, suspended in time. The catch fence caught the airborne car, slowing it before throwing it back toward the track. It landed on its right sidepod, then, in a blur, barrel rolled—three, four, five times—down the front stretch, before coming to rest upside down, steaming and broken.

"We've had a horrible crash here at qualifying for the Indianapolis 500." Buxton's excited tone contained a sharp note of uneasy concern. "Eric Simms, driver of the Red Alert-sponsored Dallara, has crashed coming out of turn four."

"That was a hard, hard hit by Simms," Hinchcliffe said. "We can only hope that he is all right and that he walks away from this accident."

The television feed showed emergency crews rushing toward the twisted wreckage of Simms's heavily damaged car. Simms was motionless in the cockpit, his body slumped sideways against the aeroscreen.

Mike Bedrosian's voice broke through the silence. "Eric, are you all right?"

"Eric, can you hear me?"

"Are you okay?"

CHAPTER 2

Reporters packed into the tiny meeting room at Indianapolis Methodist Hospital, their murmurs rising, filling the air with an uneasy buzz.

Several chairs were packed together in the small room, their metallic frames squeaking occasionally as a reporter shifted to get more comfortable. A simple table sat on a small riser, and behind the table sat two empty chairs, stiff and functional. A banner with the hospital's logo was prominently displayed on the front of the table, its colors bright against the muted tone of the room. On top of the table sat two microphones and two bottles of water.

When he entered the room, Dr. James Ferris adjusted his glasses, the light catching the lenses and momentarily reflecting off. He surveyed the room of assembled reporters, their eyes trained on him, their pens poised over their notebooks. The sight of the crowd unsettled him, and for a brief moment, he considered retreating. He sat and adjusted the microphone in front of him, the sound of it echoing slightly in the quiet room. Another man sat beside him, noisily scooting his chair up to the table. Dr. Ferris glanced at the man. *Do I look that nervous?* he wondered.

A man dressed in a fashionable blue suit and red tie stepped to the lectern next to the table, his voice crisp and practiced. "Hello, and thank you all for coming. My name is Brian DeLap of IndyCar Communications, and we have two people here today to speak about the terrible accident that occurred yesterday during qualifying for the Indianapolis 500." His words were measured, his tone carrying the serious weight of the moment. "We have Dr. James Ferris from Indianapolis Methodist Hospital with us today, as well as the owner of Catalyst Racing, Clint Harbon. Dr. Ferris, why don't you get us started?"

Dr. Ferris straightened in his seat, shifting uncomfortably as he adjusted the microphone once again. He cleared his throat, the sharpness of the action causing a small twinge of discomfort in his chest. "Good morning. My name is Dr. James Ferris. I'm a neurologist and trauma surgeon here at Indianapolis Methodist Hospital. I'm one of the doctors treating Eric Simms following his accident yesterday at the Indianapolis Motor Speedway." His voice was steady, but the words felt foreign as they left his mouth. He was used to the stress of the operating room, the steady beep of heart monitors and the controlled chaos of surgery, not the glaring spotlight of a press conference.

He paused for a moment and took a drink from the plastic water bottle that had been sitting near his microphone. It was warm, the bottle slightly crinkled, and he wondered if it had been placed there for him or if it had been left behind by someone else. The warm water was far from refreshing, but he took another sip just the same. He cleared his throat again, feeling his heart rate increase.

"Mr. Simms arrived yesterday and was immediately evaluated in the ER where it was determined that he had a nondisplaced fractured cervical vertebra in his neck at the C7 level, as well as a fractured skull." Dr. Ferris' voice was calm as he recited the details. "He was unconscious when he arrived. We immobilized his neck to prevent any further injury, and we installed a stent in his head to relieve pressure from the swelling in his brain. We also sedated Mr. Simms to aid in the healing process, and we continue to keep him in a drug-induced coma. It is anticipated that he will remain in a coma for two or three days until the swelling in his brain goes down."

Dr. Ferris took a deep breath, the weight of the words settling on the gathered crowd. He glanced at the man sitting to his left and gave him a small nod.

Clint Harbon, dressed in a button-down shirt, the logos of his team's sponsors emblazoned across the chest in a patchwork of corporate support, pulled the microphone closer, adjusting it so it rested comfortably in front of him. He looked out at the sea of reporters, his palms clammy, his fingers curling around the edge of the microphone stand.

"Good morning." Clint's Texas-accented voice was flat, the words hanging in the air for a moment before he continued. He felt the awkwardness seep into his tone, as if each syllable was somehow too much to bear. He didn't want to be here. Not now, not under these circumstances.

"My name is Clint Harbon. H-A-R-B-O-N," he said, automatically spelling his name, as if he was being questioned in a deposition. He quickly regretted it. No one had asked him to spell his name. He sighed. "I'm the owner of Catalyst Racing, the team that Eric Simms drives for. Yesterday's accident was a horrible event, and everyone at Catalyst Racing is praying for a full and speedy recovery for Eric."

Clint's fingers tightened on the edge of the microphone stand, and he kept his gaze downward. He didn't want to look at the reporters, didn't want to see their faces full of judgment, full of pity. He just wanted to get through this.

"Yesterday's accident was caused when the left front upright suffered a catastrophic failure," Clint said, the words heavy on his tongue. "The accident wasn't Eric's fault. We don't know what led to the upright failure, but there was nothing Eric could have done to avoid the accident."

There. The words were out, and he couldn't take them back. Now the reporters and the fans had their answers. They'd blame him, blame the team, even though they hadn't done anything wrong. If they wanted a culprit, they should blame the manufacturer of the part. But that's not how things worked. He shifted in his seat, feeling the weight of the reporters' eyes.

"After consulting with Red Alert and the other sponsors on Eric's car, we have decided to withdraw the entry and sit out this year's Indianapolis 500," Clint said. "Again, we wish Eric a full and speedy recovery."

He pushed the microphone away, feeling a sense of relief. He had said what he needed to say, and now he wanted to retreat back into the shadows.

Thank you both very much," DeLap said. "Does anyone have any questions for Dr. Ferris or Clint Harbon?" Several hands shot up from the crowd. Brian pointed at one of the reporters.

"Yes, Terry, go ahead."

"Dr. Ferris, do you expect Eric to make a full recovery, or do you expect him to have some lingering issues?"

"It's too early to say for sure." Dr. Ferris' tone was even, but with an underlying hesitation. "We'll know more in a day or two. Maybe three. Once the swelling goes down, we'll have a much clearer picture of Eric's injuries and prognosis."

Brian nodded and called on another reporter.

"Doctor, can you say if Eric will walk again once he's healed, and if so, will he ever be able to race in IndyCar again?"

Dr. Ferris adjusted the microphone closer to his mouth. "The fracture of Eric's cervical vertebrae is nondisplaced, and there was no impact to the spinal cord. Although he was unconscious, we ran tests that indicated Eric has feeling in his extremities, and he can move his legs and feet. I don't expect him to have any issues walking in the future."

Dr. Ferris paused. He blinked and refocused. "I'm sorry. What was the other part of your question?"

"Will Eric be able to drive race cars in the future?" the reporter repeated.

"That's right," Dr. Ferris said, remembering the question now. "It's too soon to say for sure. Again, we'll know more in a few days once the swelling goes down."

"Brady, you're next," DeLap said, pointing to one of the reporters.

Brady Collins, the main IndyCar reporter for the *Indianapolis Star*, raised his hand with a practiced air of confidence. He was known for his sharp questions and his relentless ability to dig deep. He was respected by some within IndyCar, hated by others, because he was always searching for an angle he could exploit or a scandal he could expose.

"Clint, who will you be putting in the car moving forward until Eric is ready to reclaim his seat?" Brady asked.

Clint's jaw clenched at the phrasing. "Reclaim" was too loaded, too suggestive of conflict where none existed. Brady was already trying to cause problems.

"We don't know who's going to take over the car, Brady," Clint replied, his tone clipped. "Hell, the accident just happened yesterday. But once Eric is ready to race again—and I'm certain he will be ready to race again—the seat is his. He's earned it."

That should shut up that little SOB, Clint thought. He pushed his chair back from the table, God, he was ready to go home.

Chapter 3

Dr. Ferris stood next to Eric's bed, his gaze drifting briefly to the green, rhythmic line of the heart monitor. Eric's mother, Connie, sat in a chair beside the bed, her posture rigid with worry. At the end of the bed stood Eric's girlfriend, Michelle, who watched Dr. Ferris, her eyes expectant and filled with judgement. Eric remained in a deep, drug-induced coma, but after three long days, the doctor had decided the swelling in his brain had subsided enough to safely bring him out of it.

"Will it take long?" Connie asked, her voice tight with anxiety. She sat up, readying herself for his answer.

"We're slowly weaning him off the sedatives, so it isn't a quick process," Dr. Ferris said. "It could be an hour or two before he comes to."

Connie nodded, subconsciously clutching the edge of her seat.

"I need to make some phone calls," Michelle said. She gave Connie a brief look before heading for the door. "I'll be in the waiting room."

"She seems disappointed," Dr. Ferris said, noting the abruptness of Michelle's departure.

"She's always in a hurry, doing ten things at once. She's not one to sit still." Connie stood, though she wasn't sure why. "I'll let her know when Eric wakes up."

Dr. Ferris turned his attention to the nurse, who was adjusting Eric's IV drip, keeping a close watch on his vitals. "Please let me know when he regains consciousness."

"Yes, doctor," the nurse said, her voice professional and respectful.

"I'll be just down the hall if you need me." Dr. Ferris nodded to Connie, then turned to leave.

Connie slumped into the chair beside the bed, her body collapsing under the weight of the last few days, not just from the endless hours spent in the hospital, but from the slow, constant ache in her chest that she had been carrying since the moment of Eric's accident. This was the part of his career she feared the most. But she could never bring herself to try to talk him out of racing. It was Eric's life, and he loved it more than anything. Even so, there was a part of her, a dark, selfish part, that hoped this accident would be the wake-up call Eric needed to leave racing behind and find a safer career.

Connie closed her eyes for just a moment, the fatigue pulling at her as she drifted off into a light sleep. She had only gotten two or three hours of sleep the previous night, staying late at the hospital and returning early that morning. But at least she was here, in Indianapolis, where the medical care was world-class and where she could sleep in her own bed at night. That small comfort kept her grounded, even as she was consumed with worry about her son.

They had lived near Fort Lauderdale, in Pembroke Pines, when Eric was born. After Connie divorced Eric's father, Martin, she and Eric rented an apartment in Stuart, Florida, about an hour and a half north of their former home. It was there that Eric had first taken to karting, his passion for racing ignited. The sport was expensive, and Connie struggled to make ends meet with her job as a court reporter and the meager child support payments Martin paid each month. But Eric had a gift for racing, and he was determined to make a career of it.

A week after graduating high school, Eric moved to Europe to race in the Formula BMW series. Connie had taken out a second mortgage to fund Eric's dream of a career in Formula 1, though the money barely covered his first year. She had explained to him that there would be no more money after that. Eric took the news in stride. "I'll just have to do well enough to attract sponsors."

In his first year in Europe, Eric won eight out of fifteen Formula BMW races and earned a seat in the GP3 series, a step closer to his dream of racing in Formula 1. Connie helped as much as she could with food and lodging, but money was tight and there wasn't always enough to send him. After five wins in GP3, Eric had been chosen to race in the GP2 series with one of the top teams, but he was still far from making money. He was, however, on the edge of the biggest opportunity of his career.

Eric won four of the first ten races in GP2, but a broken foot from an accident at Hockenheimring in Germany sidelined him for the rest of the season. Connie could still hear the fear in his voice when he called her, telling her about the accident and expressing his worry that his career had come to an end. He'd been in the hunt for the GP2 championship, but sitting out the remainder of the season meant he couldn't finish in the top five, let alone win the championship.

Even then, despite the sting of disappointment, Connie pushed her own doubts aside and encouraged Eric. She told him, as she always did, that things would work out. And they did, at least for him.

Eric was hired by Rototech Formula 1 as a test driver, a position that came with a seat in GP2 and another shot at the championship. He ultimately finished second, just ten points shy of the title, but his performance was good enough to move him up to become Rototech's reserve driver, attending races and waiting for his chance to get into the Formula 1 car. Over the course of three seasons, that chance never came.

When Eric was frustrated, it was Connie who became his sounding board. She encouraged him, even when her heart ached at the thought of him chasing a dream that might never come true.

She had been relieved when Eric called, telling her he was stepping away from his Formula 1 dream and returning to the U.S. to race in IndyCar. He wasn't giving up racing, but at least he would be closer to home. For Connie, that felt like a small victory.

When Eric moved to Indianapolis, Connie decided to move too. She had grown tired of the oppressive Florida heat, tired of the staleness of her job. Eric's move was the nudge she needed to start a new life.

From the moment she arrived, Indianapolis felt like home. She had given up court reporting, gotten her real estate license, and started a new career. Eric's success in IndyCar had enabled him to help her buy a new house, a symbol of his gratitude for all she had done for him. Every time she thought of that moment, Eric's words made her tear up. "It's the least I can do after everything you've done for me."

Connie stared out the hospital room window, watching cars enter and leave the parking lot, thinking about what the future might hold for her son, when he woke from his coma.

"Florence, can you get me some water?" Eric's words were sluggish, his voice hoarse and strained, as if he spoke through a mixture of gravel and fog.

Connie turned sharply. *Florence? Who was Florence?* she wondered.

"It's me, Eric. It's Mom." Her heart leapt in her chest at the sound of his voice.

"Can you get him a glass of water?" the nurse asked. "I'll get Dr. Ferris."

Connie quickly poured a glass of water and helped Eric sip from the straw, her hands trembling as she did. After a few sips, Eric pulled away, exhausted.

"How are you feeling?" She placed her hand gently on his shoulder.

"I'm tired," he said, his voice thick with sleep. "Where am I? What happened?"

Before she could answer, Dr. Ferris entered, his presence a welcome relief. "Welcome back," he said to Eric, offering a brief but reassuring smile. "You gave us quite a scare. How are you feeling?"

"I feel like I could sleep for a week."

"You've already been asleep for three days, so only four more to go."

Dr. Ferris' attempt at humor fell flat, the weight of the situation thick in the air.

"What do you mean?" Eric's eyes narrowed in confusion. "What happened?"

"I'm sorry, Eric. I sometimes forget that my patients don't know what I know," Dr. Ferris said. "You're at Indianapolis Methodist Hospital. You were brought here after you were involved in a qualifying accident for the Indy 500. Do you remember the accident?"

Eric's brow knitted together in concentration. "No, the last thing I remember was putting on my helmet and getting into the car on pit road."

"That was three days ago," Dr. Ferris said. "You've been in a drug-induced coma since then. You suffered a traumatic brain injury, which resulted in swelling in your brain. We put you in a coma to allow your body to heal. The swelling is down now, and you're out of the woods. You still have a lot of healing to do, but the hard part is over."

"When can I race again?" Eric asked.

Connie inhaled audibly, concern flickering in her eyes. Dr. Ferris met her gaze before returning his attention to Eric.

"We don't know that yet," Dr. Ferris said. "It's going to take some time for you to heal. Between us here at the hospital and IndyCar Medical, you'll be treated and evaluated. It will be up to IndyCar Medical to determine when you're ready to return to racing."

Eric paused, processing the information, then asked, "Will I be ready for the 500?"

Dr. Ferris let out a light chuckle, trying to ease the tension. "Not this year's 500." His demeanor sobered. "You need to be patient, Eric. You've suffered serious injuries, and it's going to take time to get back into a position where you can race again. I know it's only May, but I don't think you'll be ready to race this season. You need to rest, and when the time comes, we'll get you into physical therapy and eventually back into the gym."

Eric's frustration was palpable. "Do you know what caused the accident? Did I do something wrong?" He glanced between his mother and Dr. Ferris, a hint of fear in his eyes.

"Clint said your left front upright collapsed," Connie said, her voice steady. "There was nothing you could have done."

Her words brought Eric some relief. His shoulders relaxed. At least he wasn't to blame for the accident. "This is like that time I got thrown from a horse and hit my head," he said. "I couldn't remember it happening afterwards."

Dr. Ferris patted him gently on the shoulder. "I'll be back to check on you soon." As he stepped toward the door, Michelle entered, her face lighting up when she saw Eric awake.

"Oh my God, you're awake." Michelle's voice trembled with emotion.

Eric smiled weakly, his eyes still heavy with sleep.

"How are you feeling?" Michelle asked, her tone tender as she leaned in, mindful of the cervical collar around Eric's neck.

"Great," he said, though his voice lacked its usual energy. "How about you?"

Michelle laughed softly, then gave Eric a gentle hug.

"When did you fall off a horse?" Connie asked, her curiosity piqued.

"Out west in Nebraska Territory." Eric's voice was weak and laced with confusion. "Or maybe in Colorado?" He spoke slowly, unsurely.

Connie frowned, glancing at Michelle. "Do you know anything about him falling off a horse in Colorado?" she asked, concern creeping into her voice.

"No," Michelle said. "When did that happen?"

"I was breaking a horse for Rachel," Eric said, his words trailing off as if the memory was slipping through his fingers. "The horse bucked me off. I hit my head and didn't remember a thing about it afterwards."

"Who's Rachel?" Michelle asked, her voice tinged with jealousy.

Eric's face contorted as he tried to grasp the details. "She was…I'm not sure."

"You should get some rest," the nurse said gently, stepping into the conversation. She turned her attention to Connie and Michelle. "Maybe you can talk about this when he wakes up."

CHAPTER 4

Eric woke with a dull, throbbing pain in his head and a dryness in his throat, as if the air in the room had drained the moisture from him. He tried to clear his throat, but it felt like sandpaper against the rawness inside. His mouth was parched, his lips cracked from the lack of hydration. He winced, the light from the window blurring his vision as he tried to focus on the room around him.

"Do you need water?" his mother asked. Her voice was like a balm to the discomfort that pulsed in his skull.

Eric tried to speak, to tell her that yes, he needed water, but the sound that escaped his throat was less a word and more a croak, a rasping, indecipherable noise. He nodded slightly, the movement stiff with the neck brace that confined his head.

Connie, ever the caretaker, quickly filled a cup with cool water and held it in front of him, helping him maneuver the straw to his mouth. The coldness of the water provided instant relief, smoothing the rough edges in his throat. He took the cup from her hands, his grip tentative, drinking a little more before returning it.

"How are you feeling today?" she asked. Her voice was tinged with concern but held the warmth of a mother's devotion.

"My head hurts." He spoke slowly, each word seeming to drag itself out. "It seems worse than yesterday."

Connie placed the cup of water on the table in the corner of the room, then settled into the chair beside the bed. She sighed quietly, manifesting the weight of her worry. "They're weaning you off the pain medication. But the nurse said if the pain gets too bad, they can give you more."

"It's okay for now," Eric replied, his voice hoarse. He didn't want more medication. He wanted clarity.

"I want to ask you something," She searched his face. "Yesterday, you mentioned falling off a horse in Colorado. Do you remember that?"

Eric nodded slightly, the motion stiff and slow. It felt like it took all his energy just to move his head. "I do," he said, the memory flickering like a faint candlelight in the back of his mind.

"When did that happen?" she asked.

He frowned, his eyes narrowing, as he stared at the ceiling, trying to piece the memory together. "I remember it was out west," he said slowly, his voice still rough. "I want to say it was in the Nebraska Territory, but that doesn't make sense. Maybe it was Colorado, but I don't think I've ever ridden a horse in Colorado." He shook his head, chuckling quietly to himself, though it sounded more like a sigh. "I don't know. It's like… trying to remember a dream."

"How can you remember something that never happened?" Connie asked.

"I don't know," Eric said. His voice trailed off as the confusion clouded his mind. "I remember it, but I don't think it happened, at least not to me."

Connie's eyes softened with concern, but there was an edge of curiosity as well. "When you first came out of the coma, you called me Florence."

Eric nodded, the name cutting through the haze in his mind. "I remember."

"Who's Florence?" Connie asked. She reached out to adjust the blanket on his bed, though the movement was as much for her own comfort as it was for his.

Eric smiled, the corners of his mouth twitching nervously. "That's even weirder."

"What do you mean?" Her gaze was intense, searching her son's face for answers she was afraid to hear.

"I know this doesn't make sense," he said. "But Florence is my sister."

Connie's breath caught in her throat, and for a moment, the world seemed to stand still. "You don't have a sister."

"I know," he said, his own confusion deepening. "And to make things even more complicated, you're Florence."

Connie raised her hand to her mouth, as if to stifle the rising panic inside. "I'm Florence?"

"I don't know, Mom," Eric said. "There are a bunch of weird thoughts going through my head. I don't understand what's going on."

Connie placed her hand on Eric's shoulder, a soft, comforting gesture she hoped could ease his burden. "I shouldn't have brought it up," she said. "Don't let it bother you. You hit your head hard in the crash. I'm sure this is normal. Just put it out of your mind and I'll talk to the doctor about it."

A deep unease twisted in Eric's chest. He couldn't simply *put it out of his mind*. These new memories weren't like regular memories. They were flashes—vivid and real—appearing suddenly, then vanishing just as quickly, leaving him grasping for something just beyond his reach.

CHAPTER 5

The hospital room was dark, the soft beeps and buzzes of machines a constant companion as Eric did his best to sleep. Every time he drifted off, a nurse would come to check his vitals, the click of the door cutting through the quiet like a sharp blade. Each time, he felt his body lurch back to wakefulness, frustrated by the interruptions. Ironically, the hospital, a place meant for rest and healing, was the least restful place he could imagine.

As the minutes dragged on, the darkness of the room seemed to deepen, swallowing him whole as he fought to find the rest his body desperately needed. Finally, his eyelids grew heavy. But just as he was about to succumb to the welcoming embrace of unconsciousness, his mind betrayed him. Vivid images flickered in his mind, fragments of memories that weren't his.

At first, he couldn't place the images. But as they came into focus, he realized with an unsettling clarity that they were glimpses of other people's lives—memories that didn't belong to him, yet occupied space in his head.

He was standing at a construction site, surrounded by the dull gray of overcast skies. The air was cool, the chill biting at his skin. Though he couldn't see himself, he felt as if he was looking through someone else's eyes, feeling the subtle weight of a hammer in his hand. He was driving nails into a wooden frame, the sound of the hammer hitting the nail sharp and precise, each strike reverberating through his arm. He didn't know how he knew what to do, but somehow it felt instinctive, like he had done it a thousand times before. He was building a wall, carefully and expertly joining pieces of wood together.

Eric tried to look around, his gaze darting to the edges of the scene, but the image shifted again before he could make sense of it. The construction site was gone.

Now, he was running. The ground beneath him felt uneven, rough under his boots. He was surrounded by men—soldiers in uniform. They carried backpacks and rifles, the weight of their gear slowing them, dragging them down. The scene was frantic, the urgency palpable. The men in front of him moved quickly, and he, too, ran toward a wall. As he got closer, he saw one of the men in front of him climb over the wall with ease, his movements practiced and swift. There were only two men left between him and the barrier.

Eric felt the weight of the rifle pulling on his shoulders, the strain making every movement more difficult. The backpack strapped to his shoulders pressed into his back, slowing him as he pushed forward. His heavy boots were stiff and unwieldy, hampering his ability to run.

A man with a gruff voice stood next to the wall, yelling at the soldiers, encouraging them on. "Pick up the pace, you sorry sons a bitches. Get moving. Get over that wall."

Now, it was his turn to climb the wall. He jumped, grabbing the top, but the weight of the gear made it harder than it should have been. He struggled, pulling himself up, feeling the strain in his arms and legs as he tried to hoist his body over the wall. When he finally managed to get a foot over the top, he summoned what little strength he had left and hoisted himself up and over the wall, landing with a thud on the other side. The impact reverberated in his bones, knocking the breath out of him.

Before he could fully process the sensation, he was in a kitchen, the malty sweet aroma of tea filling the air. There was a stillness, an old-world quality to the room. He held a delicate porcelain cup, the pale blue pattern that circled the rim intricate and beautiful. The weight of the cup felt unfamiliar, and fragile in his hands.

He carefully poured the tea, making sure not to spill a single drop, an odd sense of anxiety settling over him. There was an overwhelming need to be gentle with the cup, as though the tea itself was fragile, its contents precious. When the cup was full, he placed the kettle back on the stove and gently lifted the cup and saucer, holding them with both hands as if afraid that even the slightest jostle might ruin something.

He moved toward a large, wooden door, the sound of the floorboards creaking beneath his steps. As he pushed through the door, he entered an adjoining room, where an old man, his hair a mass of thin gray strands, sat in a chair. The man's eyes fluttered open, his face creased with age and irritation. He grabbed a thick wooden cane from beside him and rapped it on the floor, the sound startling.

"Damn you, Hopper," the man said, his voice thick with a sharp English accent. He rapped the cane against the floor again, the sound echoing through the room.

Eric—or whoever he was—closed his eyes, bracing himself for the expected strike. The tension in his body coiled tight, waiting. He felt the sensation of his body rocking back and forth, but there was no impact. The expected blow never came. He waited a moment longer before he cautiously opened his eyes.

When he did, he was outside, surrounded by the vast expanse of nature. The grass was soft beneath him, long wisps of green and brown stretching out toward the horizon. In the distance, a massive mountain range rose against the sky, its peaks obscured by a faint mist.

And then, suddenly, he realized he was on a horse. The sensation of movement was unmistakable, the rhythmic shift of his body as the horse moved through the grass. It wasn't just the horse's motion he felt, but the sensation of being in someone else's body.

He shifted in the saddle, and as he did, a deep sadness washed over him. He wasn't sure what caused the sadness, but the weight of it was unbearable. Tears welled up, blurring his view of the mountains. He wiped them with his sleeve, but they kept streaming down his cheeks. There was no one else around, no sound of human voices, just the endless stretch of grass and the silence of the wild.

The horse moved steadily toward the mountains, and Eric—or the person whose eyes he was seeing through—felt an overwhelming grief, a loss that went beyond understanding. Not just sadness, devastation. Something terrible had happened, though he could not grasp what it was.

He reached up and touched the brim of a hat, his fingers brushing against the worn fabric. As he glanced down, he saw his legs, clothed in wool pants that were weathered from use, and boots with worn heels that held his feet firmly in the stirrups. His shirt was long-sleeved and brown, partially covered by a vest.

Tears continued to fall, soaking into his clothes, the horse's coat, and the earth beneath them. Whatever had happened, it had left a hole too vast to understand.

He wiped his eyes again, and as he did, the scene dissolved, starting from the edges and moving inward. The mountains, the grass, the vastness of the landscape, all faded into darkness.

Before the darkness consumed him, a word rose from his throat, almost as if it had been waiting there all along. He whispered it, barely audible: "Rachel."

Chapter 6

Connie paced in the hallway outside Eric's room, her hands clasped tightly in front of her as she stared down at the floor. The sterile, pale walls of the hospital seemed to close in on her as she paced slowly, lost in thought.

What if the trauma from Eric's accident caused a permanent brain injury and he would never be able to care for himself again? What if these strange memories began to take over his life and personality? Of course, if that were the case, she would take care of him. She was his mother. She had to. But fear gnawed at her. Was it wrong to not want to shoulder that burden? Did that make her a bad mother?

The sound of footsteps pulled her out of her internal struggle and snapped her back to the present. Dr. Ferris walked toward her, his coat rustling softly with each step, his glasses reflecting the harsh, artificial light. He seemed to carry an air of calm authority, yet there was something humanizing about the tiredness in his eyes.

"How's our favorite driver today?" Dr. Ferris asked, a slight smile forming.

"I'm not sure," Connie said. "He's having some pain in his head, but there's something else too."

"The pain is easy to deal with," he said. "What else is going on?"

Connie hesitated, unsure of how to put her concerns into words. She took a deep breath, feeling the cool, sterile air fill her lungs. She spoke slowly, choosing each word carefully. "I'm not sure how to say it. He seems to have memories of things that never happened to him. Yesterday, he mentioned to you that he'd once fallen off a horse and struck his head."

"I remember."

"Except he's never fallen off a horse." Connie's voice was tight with confusion and concern. "He says he remembers it happening in the Nebraska Territory or maybe Colorado, but he also remembers that he's never ridden a horse in Colorado."

"The Nebraska Territory?" The question hung in the air for a beat. "That is strange."

"There's more." Connie grappled with the weight of what she was about to say. She paused for a moment, not wanting to sound irrational. "He says he has a sister named Florence, but he's also aware that he's an only child." She didn't mention that Eric had also said she was his sister—that felt too strange to speak aloud.

Dr. Ferris removed his glasses and wiped the lens with the edge of his lab coat, then put his glasses back on. "It's possible Eric suffered a brain injury that is making him confused about past events, people, and places. Being confused, even forgetful, after an accident like Eric experienced would not be uncommon. But it would be highly unusual for a brain injury to create memories that never actually happened. That's something I've never encountered."

"Do you think it could be permanent?" Her voice cracked slightly with the weight of her question.

"That's hard to say." His tone was soft and measured. "At this point, I'm really not sure what we're dealing with."

"I'm just afraid…" Connie hesitated, her chest tightening. "I'm worried he's not going to be the Eric I've known his whole life." Tears welled up in her eyes, her breath catching in her throat as she fought to keep herself composed. The weight of her fear made it hard to breathe.

Dr. Ferris looked at her, his expression softening. "I understand your concern," he said. "For now, it's probably best to put those worries out of your mind and stay as positive as you can. Traumatic brain injuries can be hard to predict, and Eric has a lot of healing to do. Let's see how things progress before we start fearing the worst."

Connie wiped her eyes and took a deep, shaky breath. She knew Dr. Ferris was right. She needed to focus on the present, on helping Eric heal, not on what might or might not happen. She nodded, feeling the weight of her emotions, but trying to remain strong. "You're right," she said. "Positive attitude." She gave her best attempt at a smile, though it felt more like a mask than a true expression of hope.

"Let's go in to see Eric, shall we?" Dr. Ferris said, motioning for Connie to follow him. He stepped forward, and she followed, her footsteps quiet on the tile corridor floor. As they entered Eric's room, they found him awake, sitting up in bed, his posture more alert than before.

"How are you feeling?" Dr. Ferris asked. His tone was warm and professional. "Your mother said you had some pain in your head."

"It's actually better now," Eric said. His voice was a little stronger, but the weariness was still evident.

"If it gets bad again, let us know and we can give you something for it."

Eric nodded, though there was an undercurrent of frustration in his eyes, as if he wanted nothing more than to move past the pain and get back to his life.

"I want to ask you some questions," Dr. Ferris continued. "They're just general knowledge questions and they shouldn't be too hard for you. Are you ready?"

"Sure, ask away."

Dr. Ferris asked the month, the year, the name of the president, and other simple questions designed to test Eric's awareness and understanding of the present. Eric answered them easily, his responses coming without hesitation.

"Good." Dr. Ferris nodded approvingly. "Now I want to ask you about some of these memories you're having. Let's start with the time you fell off the horse in Colorado."

Eric looked down, his expression faltering. "It's hard to explain. I want to say it happened in the Nebraska Territory, but that doesn't make sense. It could have been Colorado." He cleared his throat. "I don't actually remember falling off the horse, but I remember being told about it afterwards. I was riding the horse, and the next thing I remember, I was in bed with a cold rag on my head. But even as I say that, I know I've never gone horseback riding in Colorado, and I wasn't around when the Nebraska Territory was a thing."

The discomfort in Eric's voice was palpable, and Connie felt her heart tighten with concern. She could hear the confusion, the dissonance in his words, and it made her want to reach out and reassure him.

The memory made Eric uneasy, and he quickly tried to shift the conversation. "Do you have any idea how long it will be until I can get back into a race car?" he asked. His tone was casual, but there was an underlying edge to his voice.

"I suspect it will be months," Dr. Ferris replied. "You suffered a severe head injury and a broken neck. We want to make sure you are completely recovered before you get back behind the wheel."

Eric's shoulders slumped, the weight of his frustration showing clearly on his face. "Months?" he muttered under his breath.

"You say you were told about the horseback riding accident after it happened. Who told you?" Dr. Ferris asked, steering the conversation back to the memory.

Eric exhaled deeply, his eyes shifting uneasily between his mother and the doctor. He hesitated, as if he didn't want to voice what had been lingering in his mind. Finally, his voice came out in a whisper, almost as though he were reluctant to speak the name aloud. "Rachel told me."

"And who is Rachel?" Dr. Ferris asked.

Eric glanced at his mother, his eyes filled with uncertainty. "She was my wife."

Chapter 7

Michelle tapped her foot impatiently, the movement sharp and quick. "How can you have a memory about your wife if you've never been married?" Her voice had a tight edge to it, the words vibrating with frustration.

"I don't know, Michelle." Eric's voice was soft but tinged with the same confusion that had plagued him for days. "I don't understand any of this." He shifted slightly in the bed, trying to get comfortable, but the tension of the conversation hung in the air like a storm cloud.

For fifteen minutes, Michelle had asked him the same question in different ways. She wanted to know everything about Rachel, her relentless questioning wearing him thin. Her gaze, which was usually caring and supportive, now felt sharp and demanding, as if she were clinging to the hope that he would provide her with an answer that didn't exist.

Most of the time, Eric admired her persistent approach to life. When she set her mind on a goal, she didn't let go until she achieved it. That was one of the things that drew him to her. But Michelle's persistence also had a dark side. She could be single-minded and unable to let go of something better left alone.

They had met in the paddock of an IndyCar race at Road America. Michelle was a public relations representative for one of the teams, her presence as smooth and polished as her ability to navigate the fast-paced world of motorsport. They struck up a conversation, and Eric learned that Michelle had recently started her own one-woman PR firm. Later that weekend, they ran into each other at Siebkens, a bar near the track in Elkhart Lake. They had been together ever since.

Michelle wasn't like the women Eric had dated previously. She was driven, self-assured, and confident in her opinions. Michelle believed there were absolute rights and wrongs in life, and she could be hypercritical of others when they did what she believed was wrong. But she could also be caring and supportive. That was the side of Michelle's personality Eric focused on, and the side that endeared her to him.

"I just don't see how you can…" Her words trailed off as she searched for another angle.

Dr. Ferris walked in just as Michelle's voice rose again, his entrance a welcome interruption. The sound of the door creaking open felt like a release, breaking the tension that had been building between them.

"Good morning," Dr. Ferris said. "How are you today, Eric?"

"I'm feeling okay, but my head is full of other people's memories." Eric's tone was weary and frustrated.

"More than before?" Dr. Ferris asked.

"A lot more." He met Dr. Ferris' eyes hopefully, searching for answers. "Is this something that can happen with brain injuries?"

Dr. Ferris shifted slightly, his hands clasped in front of him as he took a moment to consider the question. "What you're experiencing is not a common occurrence after suffering a brain injury." His voice was calm but laced with a hint of uncertainty. "That's not to say it can't happen. There's a lot we don't understand about the brain. But I've never run across anything like what you're experiencing."

"I'm remembering other people's lives like they're my own." The words tumbled out in a rush. The strange memories suffocated him, crowding his thoughts. "This isn't like my imagination, like they're stories I'm making up. I can tell the difference between real life and made-up stories. These are real-life memories, just like my memories of talking to you yesterday."

"That must be a strange feeling."

Michelle, unable to hold her thoughts any longer, cut in sharply. "Is he going to be okay? Can you fix him?" Her voice was thick with worry, punctuated with impatience.

Dr. Ferris paused, his face clouded with thought. "That's hard to say," he said. "I'm not sure if there's anything to fix. What Eric is experiencing is unusual, but he might wake up tomorrow and have forgotten all these memories. This might turn out to be just a blip on the radar. But even if the memories don't go away, that doesn't necessarily mean that something is wrong that needs to be fixed."

"But this could sideline his career," Michelle said. The volume of her voice increased. The words hung in the air, and Eric could feel the tension rise again. It was a reality they all had to face, but it wasn't Michelle's place to bring it up, or Dr. Ferris' burden to calm her fears.

Dr. Ferris' gaze flickered between Michelle and Eric before offering a carefully measured response. "I think the best we can do is give this some time and see how it resolves."

Michelle's frustration barely hid behind a forced sigh. She opened her mouth to say more, but before she could, Dr. Ferris' voice broke the momentary silence.

"On a different topic, I have some good news. I'm going to release you from the hospital tomorrow. You still have a lot of healing to do, but you can do that at home. We're going to set you up with physical therapy, and you'll need to follow up with IndyCar medical once you're healed enough to get back in a race car. I'd also like you to follow up with a colleague of mine, Dr. Carly Pellegrino. She may be able to help you with these memories you're having. Her number will be in your discharge paperwork. She's expecting your call."

Eric looked up at Dr. Ferris, his curiosity piqued. "I'll give her a call as soon as I get home." A slight sense of relief flickered in his chest at the news there was someone who might be able to help.

Chapter 8

Dr. Pellegrino's office was in a converted single-family home, nestled in a quiet neighborhood near the hospital. The office was tucked away in a corner of the neighborhood, a stark contrast to the clinical, sterile feel of the hospital. When Michelle pulled the car into the small parking lot, she gasped.

"What the hell?" she said. "Did you see that sign?"

"What sign?" Eric asked, confused at her outburst.

"In front of the office," she said. Her eyes narrowed. "It said 'Center for Past Life Research.' They think you're some kind of wacko." Her voice carried a sharp edge.

"Past Life Research?" There was a mix of disbelief and curiosity in his voice.

Michelle parked and turned toward him, the engine still running. "You're not going to go in there, are you?"

"Why not?" he asked. "What harm is there in hearing what the doctor has to say?"

She turned off the ignition, her hands gripping the wheel tightly. "The harm is that there is no such thing as past lives. What kind of quack would work at such a place?"

Eric was used to Michelle sharing her deeply held opinions. "But I'd like to hear what they have to say." His voice was soft and calm. "Let's just see."

Michelle swallowed hard, considering his request. "Okay, but don't let them make a fool of you," she said.

Eric nodded, and they both got out of the car. He could feel the reluctance in Michelle's movements as they walked across the small parking lot. He reached out and took her hand in his.

Inside, the receptionist greeted them and introduced herself as Rose. Her voice was soft and pleasant, her smile warm and welcoming.

"Dr. Pellegrino will be right with you," Rose said, her soft voice like a soothing balm. The balm seemed to only irritate Michelle further.

The walls of the small, well-appointed waiting room were painted a warm shade of beige, and the lighting was gentle, a stark contrast to the harsh fluorescent lights of the hospital. Soft background music played, a gentle melody barely noticeable. The room smelled faintly of ginger and vanilla. Eric eased onto a comfortable sofa with an autumn-colored leaf pattern. Michelle sat next to him, crossing her legs and nervously tapping her foot, a rhythmic clicking sound that seemed too loud in the otherwise quiet room.

"I don't think this is a good idea, Eric." Her eyes darted toward the door, as if hoping someone might step in and stop this from happening.

Eric turned his whole body toward her, the neck brace he still wore restricting his movements. He took her hand in his. "It will be fine."

Michelle pulled her hand away and crossed her arms. She gave him a small, tight-lipped smile.

Michelle could not understand her boyfriend's naivete. At times, he could be smart and worldly, but he could also be innocent and gullible. He was too trusting. Too willing to accept the position other people put him in. If it were up to her, they would walk out of the Center for Past Life Research, never to return. And she would have a word with Dr. Ferris, admonishing him for sending them on this foolish errand.

A woman with dark, curly hair and wearing a white lab coat over a pair of dress slacks and a colorful, striped blouse entered, her footsteps light and graceful as she approached. She was younger than Eric had expected, her features soft but confident, her presence calming and in control. "I'm Dr. Pellegrino." She spoke with an English accent, crisp and friendly. "You must be Eric."

Eric stood, feeling the strain in his neck as he reached out to shake her hand. Dr. Pellegrino's grip was firm, professional yet welcoming.

"It's nice to meet you," he said. "This is Michelle."

Dr. Pellegrino offered her hand to Michelle, who reluctantly took it, her handshake a limp formality. She quickly pulled her hand away when the handshake concluded.

"If you'll follow me, we'll go back to my office." As Dr. Pellegrino turned to lead them to her office, Michelle gave Eric a menacing scowl.

"What?" Eric mouthed at her. Michelle turned her gaze to the floor as they followed Dr. Pellegrino.

The doctor's office was a large room with high ceilings, giving it a spacious, open feel. On one side, a desk sat, papers neatly stacked with precision, a small lamp casting a warm light. On the other side, a seating area was arranged with a gray fabric couch across from two matching straight-back chairs.

"Please, have a seat." Dr. Pellegrino gestured toward the couch.

Eric motioned to the couch, and Michelle reluctantly sat next to him. The couch was soft beneath them, but Michelle's body remained rigid, her arms and legs crossed tightly. Eric did his best to ignore her.

"Dr. Ferris called last week and told me that you are experiencing some memories that you can't explain." Dr. Pellegrino's tone was calm, her eyes attentive as she looked at Eric.

Before Eric could respond, Michelle spoke up, her voice sharp and accusatory. "And you think he's remembering past lives?" The question was loaded, as if she dared Dr. Pellegrino to confirm the absurdity of the situation.

Dr. Pellegrino smiled, a small, knowing smile. "I don't know yet. But it's possible that…"

"It's not possible because there's no such thing as past lives," Michelle interjected, her voice firm.

"I see." Dr. Pellegrino's tone was calm and steady, unaffected by the interruption. "Eric, is that how you feel?"

He looked at Michelle before answering, then directed his attention to Dr. Pellegrino. "About past lives?" he asked.

"Yes, are you open to the possibility, or have you already decided that's not what you're experiencing?"

Michelle turned on the couch to face him, her posture stiff, her arms crossed. Eric glanced at her before looking back at Dr. Pellegrino. "I don't know anything about past lives," he said. "It's not something I've ever looked into. But if it can help explain what I'm experiencing, I'm willing to listen."

Michelle rolled her eyes dramatically and sighed. "Are you even a real doctor?"

"I'm not a medical doctor," Dr. Pellegrino replied, her tone unruffled. "I'm a psychologist. I have a PhD in psychology, and I specialize in research into parapsychology, with an emphasis on reincarnation."

"A psychologist?" Michelle repeated, her voice dripping with skepticism. "They think you're a head case, Eric." She stood abruptly, pushing herself up off the couch. "This is ridiculous. I'll be in the car." Michelle stormed out.

"That was dramatic," Dr. Pellegrino said with a light chuckle, her tone dry. "Do you need to go after her?"

Eric smiled weakly, feeling a chuckle escape him despite the awkwardness of the moment. "No, she'll be in the car."

CHAPTER 9

With Michelle out of the room, the tension that had been clinging to the air seemed to evaporate, replaced by a quiet, unspoken relief. Eric leaned back, his shoulders relaxing for the first time since they'd entered.

"Let me start by telling you a little bit about what we do here at the Center for Past Life Research," Dr. Pellegrino said. "Primarily, we study cases of children—usually between the ages of two and eight—who are having memories they can't explain. We do most of our work with children because it's extremely unusual for an adult to have unexplained memories that are detailed enough to be investigated thoroughly."

She paused, her eyes scanning the notes on her tablet, her fingers lightly swiping through a few pages as the soft glow of the screen illuminated her face. Eric noticed how deliberate her movements were, each swipe measured, as if she was carefully organizing her thoughts.

"Dr. Ferris tells me that your memories began after you were in an automobile accident. Is that correct?"

"Well, yes," he said. "I was qualifying for the Indy 500 when my car hit the wall." He wasn't sure why he felt the need to explain it this way, but it mattered to him. He didn't want her to think it was just some minor road accident.

Dr. Pellegrino didn't react, her expression neutral, though there was a slight shift in her posture as she set the tablet down beside her on the arm of her chair, her fingers still lightly resting on it as if it were an extension of herself. "And you didn't have these memories prior to the accident?"

"That's right."

Dr. Pellegrino made a small note on her tablet, her pen scratching against the surface as it filled the quiet space between them. Then, she set the tablet aside, her hands folding neatly in her lap as she focused all her attention on Eric. "Here's what I'd like to do," she said. "I'd like you to tell me all the things you are remembering. Be as specific as possible. Once we complete our interview, I'll set out to research what you've told me. I'll conduct an investigation to determine if we can substantiate anything you're remembering. The research may bring up questions that you may or may not be able to answer. My purpose is to neither prove nor disprove the memories you're having. Rather, I want to gather as much evidence, either way, to build a case file."

Eric absorbed her words slowly, the meaning of what she was saying settling over him with a quiet weight. "You mean you aren't going to try to prove that I'm having memories of past lives?" He tried to sound casual, but there was an underlying anxiety in his voice, a need to understand where exactly this was heading.

"No, that's not my job," she said. "My job is to study what you're experiencing. It will be up to you to decide whether it involves past lives."

Eric nodded slowly, the edges of his anxiety softening just a little. "Do you believe in reincarnation?" It was a simple question, but one that had been lingering in the back of his mind since their conversation began.

Dr. Pellegrino paused, her gaze thoughtful as she considered her response. She tilted her head slightly, her eyes flicking to the window for a moment, as if the answer might be out there somewhere in the falling light coming through the blinds. "I neither believe nor disbelieve. I'm a researcher, so I conduct research and compile evidence. But this isn't the type of field where conclusions can be incontrovertibly reached. What I will say is that I'm open to the possibility. But I understand that we will likely never know for sure."

Eric appreciated her answer. She wasn't trying to force anything on him. Her candor, her calm approach, was a relief. "Okay, what questions do you have for me?" he asked.

"Before that happens, you need to agree to a series of meetings," she said. "Plus, there are forms to sign. If you're comfortable with that, I'll have you sign the forms today and we can start the interview process next week."

"Sounds good."

One more thing," Dr. Pellegrino said, her voice lowering slightly, as though it was a confidential aside. "It might be best not to bring anyone with you to our next meeting."

Eric laughed, the sound escaping from him in a soft burst of air. "Oh, I don't think she'll be back."

CHAPTER 10

Eric poured his mom a cup of coffee, the rich, warm liquid swirling gently as it filled the mug. Steam rose in soft curls, carrying with it the aroma of freshly brewed comfort. He set the cup down in front of her on the table. "Be careful, that's hot," he warned.

Connie smiled at her son, the corners of her eyes crinkling in a way that always reminded Eric of his childhood. She wrapped both hands around the cup, letting the warmth seep into her fingers. "Are you going to tell me about your visit with Dr. Pellegrino?"

Eric picked up his own cup off the kitchen counter, the ceramic mug warm against his hand. He took a slow sip as he walked to the table, the cup clinking gently as he set it down. He wore a soft neck brace now, and although his movements were still somewhat restricted, they had become more fluid. The pain in his neck and head had subsided enough so he no longer needed even over-the-counter pain medication. He felt more like himself, though he still wrestled with the strange, lingering memories.

He sat across the table from his mother. The room felt cozy. Bright morning light streamed through the kitchen window, casting long shadows and making the countertops gleam.

"It wasn't what I expected, that's for sure," he said. "Dr. Pellegrino studies past lives."

"Past lives?" Connie's eyebrows rose slightly in surprise.

"You know, reincarnation."

Connie's expression shifted, a flicker of confusion crossing her features. "What on earth does that have to do with the things you're remembering?" Her words were more an inquiry than an accusation.

"Dr. Pellegrino thinks that my memories might be from lives I've lived before." Eric took another sip of his coffee, then set the mug down slowly, looking at his mother. He knew how crazy this reincarnation theory must sound to her—how hard it must be for someone so grounded to even entertain the thought. "Sounds nuts, doesn't it?"

Connie's fingers curled around the ceramic mug she held as she thought. "I don't know. It isn't what I expected you to say, but I guess it makes some sense." She tilted her head slightly, as though the idea just started to take root.

"It does?"

Connie nodded slowly. "I mean, it could. Don't you think?" There was a trace of genuine curiosity in her eyes, a willingness to entertain the possibility, even if she couldn't fully grasp it.

Eric tilted his head, a hint of incredulousness in his voice. "You think it could be reincarnation?" Connie was one of the most level-headed, down-to-earth people he knew, someone whose feet were planted firmly on the ground. To hear her even entertain the idea of past lives surprised him.

Connie took a slow sip of her coffee, the warmth of the drink lingering as she swallowed. "Obviously, I have no way of knowing for sure, but I believe in reincarnation. I think we've all lived many lives before we were born into this one." She looked up at him, her eyes steady. "The question I have is, why are you remembering these things now?"

"Wait a minute." Eric leaned forward across the table, the motion awkward with the neck brace, but his curiosity overriding his discomfort. "You believe in reincarnation?"

"Does that surprise you?"

"I've never heard you talk about it before."

"I guess I haven't talked about it because I don't know much about it," she said. "But the concept makes sense to me." She shrugged lightly, emphasizing the ease with which she accepted the idea.

"No kidding?" Eric chuckled as he sat back in his chair. "I guess you learn something new every day."

"How did Michelle react to Dr. Pellegrino's theory?"

"Not well." Eric's voice was tinged with a mixture of frustration and humor. "She stormed out and sat in the car while I spoke to the doctor."

Connie laughed softly. "That sounds about right." She shook her head as though this behavior was something she had come to expect from Michelle.

Eric chuckled, a rueful smile on his lips. "She thinks the doctors aren't taking me seriously and that they're making a fool of me. You know how black and white she can be sometimes. Reincarnation is one of those things that are on her blacklist."

"What do you think?" she asked.

Eric sipped his coffee, warming him as he thought. Unlike Michelle, he didn't think anyone was trying to make a fool of him. At the same time, he wasn't entirely sure what to make of Dr. Pellegrino's theory. The whole thing felt surreal, like he was floating in some strange fog. His memories had gone from a curiosity to an inconvenience, occupying most hours of the day. But when he tried to access them, to see them in their entirety, they vanished. It was like trying to latch onto smoke.

"I don't know." He set the mug down on the table with a soft clink. "I have to admit that what Dr. Pellegrino said intrigues me, but I also think it sounds a little crazy. Past lives? I thought that was just something in the movies or on TV."

Connie nodded, her gaze distant for a moment as she considered his words. Eric's recovery had been a relief. Although she was still concerned about the memories he was experiencing, she was grateful that her son—the Eric she had always known—was going to be fine. These memories—whatever they were and wherever they came from—needed to be addressed. But at least her worst fears were now just a distant thought.

"Maybe it's best to keep an open mind," she said. "There's no harm in learning more. If you find talking to Dr. Pellegrino helpful, keep doing it. If not, you can always stop."

"You think I should go back to see Dr. Pellegrino?"

"Sure, don't you?" Her voice was warm and reassuring.

Eric sat back in his chair, taking in her words. "I told her I'd come back, but I've been having second thoughts. Michelle doesn't want me to see her again."

Connie smiled gently and took a sip of her coffee. "Your dad and I used to argue about reincarnation when we first started dating." She laughed at the memory. "There was very little we didn't argue about. Anyway, he was of the opinion that we live once and die. That's it. No afterlife. No reincarnation."

Eric looked up at the ceiling and sighed. "I've been meaning to ask, did Dad call after the accident?"

After Eric's parents split up, his father became more of an acquaintance than a parent, someone who popped in from time to time but never stayed long. The visits were usually strained and uncomfortable, filled with tension. Eric remembered hearing his parents fight—his mother trying to shield him from the worst of it.

"He did." Her voice was tinged with something Eric couldn't quite place. "He wanted to make sure you were okay. He said he wanted to come see you."

"What did you tell him?" A sense of hopefulness shot through Eric, then disappeared as quickly as it had arrived

"I told him that you were doing fine and that you were going to make a full recovery." Her tone was matter of fact, but there was something guarded in the way she spoke about it.

"Is he coming up from Florida?"

"No, I told him to stay home," she said. "I said that he hadn't seen you for more than a decade. There was no sense in breaking that streak now." Connie laughed softly, but Eric couldn't tell if it was humor or bitterness behind the sound.

Eric pushed ahead. "Did he sound sober?"

"He did." Connie nodded slowly. "He claims he hasn't had a drink in more than three years. I told him that was great, but it was probably still not a good idea for him to come up here to see you."

Eric nodded, his thoughts racing. "Yeah, it's probably for the best."

They sat in silence, the only sound the quiet sipping of their coffee. Eric's dad hadn't been in the picture for most of his life, and yet the part of him that wondered why his father was the way he was couldn't be quieted. But that question, that need for answers, seemed like a betrayal of his mother—of everything she had done for him.

"So, you think I should follow up with Dr. Pellegrino?" Eric asked, shifting the conversation back to something more manageable.

"Yes, I think you should."

"Then that's what I'll do."

CHAPTER 11

Eric stared at his living room wall, his posture slumped. He hadn't moved for what felt like hours, the stillness of the moment pressing in on him. The fabric of the couch was soft beneath him, but the weight of the day—of the confusion in his mind—seemed to settle on him like a heavy coat. The sun had long since dipped below the horizon, and now the early evening twilight filled the room, casting long shadows and dimming the once-vibrant living room into muted tones of blue and gray.

He didn't know what to make of the memories swirling through his head. They were fragments, disjointed and strange. He remembered being a kid living in Canada, the bitter cold seeping into his bones as he watched snow fall outside the window. He remembered being an adult in a bustling Chicago, the noise of the city vibrating through the streets and echoing in his ears. And then there was the hospital bed in England—stale sanitorium air, the murmuring of voices, and the sickening smell of decay. But who was this person, this collection of memories? Or were they just pieces of many people's lives? Each memory felt so real, so vivid, yet also impossible. Most of all, he remembered being in love with Rachel. He knew she was his wife—at least, in his memories—but he had no idea who she was or where she had gone.

With each passing day, it felt like more memories were surfacing, pressing into his consciousness with increasing urgency. He wondered—was "remembering" even the right word for this? How could you remember something that had never happened to you? But if he wasn't remembering, if these weren't memories, what exactly were they?

Dr. Ferris had once said that the memories—or whatever they were—might just go away someday. Eric hoped for that day to come as quickly as possible. He didn't have the time, nor the energy, to deal with someone else's memories taking up space in his head. He wanted a return to normal life, to heal quickly, and to get back into a race car.

But there was that nagging thought. If what he was experiencing really was a collection of his past lives, would he want to lose those memories? If reincarnation was real, and his memories were somehow tied to that, maybe remembering his past lives was a kind of gift, one that few others would ever experience.

In the short time he'd spent with Dr. Pellegrino, he had come to appreciate her approach. She was thoughtful, knowledgeable, and grounded in her methods. She didn't seem like someone who would indulge in fanciful beliefs without reason.

Truthfully, he didn't know what to make of Dr. Pellegrino. Despite Michelle's doubts, Eric found himself liking her. She was smart, and he wanted to share his memories with her to see what she made of them. But after hearing them, would she believe that he was remembering his past lives, or would she chalk it up to the trauma from the crash, just his brain making up stories to fill the void?

He laid his head back on the couch, the softness of the cushions cradling him. He closed his eyes, trying to quiet his mind, but instead, an image came into focus. It was a woman—a young woman—standing next to him. They were outside, on the porch of a log cabin. The rugged mountains loomed in the distance, their jagged peaks barely visible through a mass of dark, threatening clouds. He wanted to see her face, to hold onto the details of the moment, but the picture was blurry, like it was being obscured by fog. His heart ached with an overwhelming sense of loss and yearning. He felt her absence as if it was a tangible thing, like a hole in his chest that couldn't be filled. Was this Rachel?

A lump formed in his throat, and he opened his eyes to the dim light of the room. The scene in his mind faded as quickly as it had appeared, but the sense of loss lingered, like the echo of a song long forgotten. Had he fallen asleep? The house around him was dark now, night having fully descended.

He sat up slowly, rubbing his temples as the headache from the lingering confusion pressed against his skull. He loved this woman, whose face he couldn't see. He missed her. But how was that possible? How could he love a woman he didn't know and who only existed in his mind?

CHAPTER 12

Eric didn't know why he was nervous. He had been to the race shop many times before and enjoyed being there. But today, it felt strange to be walking into the shop unannounced, facing the team for the first time since the accident.

Eric stepped through the door expecting the usual greeting from Martha, the team's front office receptionist, but the lobby was empty. He stood for a moment, staring at the neon "Catalyst Racing" sign that hung above Martha's desk, the light flickered just slightly, casting a nostalgic glow over the otherwise lifeless room. The familiar hum of the place, the scent of oil and rubber, the echoes of the team's energy, it was all missing, replaced by an odd stillness that seemed to hang in the air. Where was everyone? With a faint sigh, he turned and made his way down the hallway to Clint's office.

He knocked on Clint's door, and a familiar voice called out, "Come in." Eric found Clint sitting at his desk, his eyes widening when he saw Eric. The tension that had been building in Eric's chest evaporated. A broad smile spread across Clint's face, and he stood quickly, offering a handshake.

"Eric, it's great to see you," Clint said, his voice genuine, and his enthusiasm palpable.

"Hi, Clint." The warmth of the handshake felt grounding, a comforting reminder of the world he was trying to return to.

"You look great," Clint said, his tone full of relief. "How are you feeling?"

"I'm good," Eric's words were honest, though there was an edge to them, a hint of frustration that he couldn't quite mask or explain. "I feel like I could get back in the car today."

Clint chuckled awkwardly, his smile fading just slightly. "That's great. Why don't you have a seat? There's something I want to talk to you about."

The chair creaked under Eric's weight as he adjusted himself. He glanced around the room, noting the familiar clutter of papers on the desk. "Where is everyone?"

"Martha has the day off, and the crew is already headed down to St. Louis," Clint said. "Gateway is this weekend." He used the track's former name, before it became Worldwide Technology Raceway.

Eric felt a wave of foolishness wash over him. He hadn't realized that the race in St. Louis was just days away. His thoughts had been so consumed by his strange memories that he'd forgotten the race schedule entirely.

"What did you want to talk to me about?" Eric asked, trying to shift the focus away from his mental lapse.

"Two things." Clint's tone shifted to something more serious. "First, I want to apologize again for the accident. I know we talked about it on the phone, but I want to say it to your face, too. The whole team feels bad about it."

Eric immediately shook his head, trying to diffuse the apology. "No one's to blame," he said. "Just a faulty part."

"But we sourced that part and put it on the car. I don't know how we would have caught it, but we should have before we installed it." Clint's voice held a quiet remorse, as though he was trying to shoulder the weight of the whole team's guilt.

Eric wasn't sure what to say. He didn't blame the team for the accident; it was just one of those things that happen sometimes in racing. But Clint seemed genuinely sorry, and Eric was grateful. "I appreciate that, Clint."

"That's the first thing." Clint sat up straighter, folding his hands on the desk in front of him, his expression becoming more professional. "I also wanted you to hear it from me that we've signed Russell Ray to take over the car for the rest of the year."

Eric felt a knot form in his stomach. Russell Ray was a rising star, a young American driver who had been dominating in the Indy NXT series; the series designed to funnel young drivers into IndyCar. He was fast, he was talented, and teams were lining up to add him to their rosters. Eric had expected Clint to hire a journeyman driver to fill the seat for the rest of the year, not someone as promising as Ray. The thought stung.

Eric did his best to keep his emotions in check, to swallow the sudden surge of panic that rose in his chest. He took a deep breath, letting it out slowly. "That's great, Clint." He forced a smile. "But I was hoping to get back in the car by the end of the season." He fought the urge to shout, *That's my seat*, but the thought simmered in the back of his mind.

"I was under the impression that you were out for the remainder of the year," Clint said, his voice carefully neutral.

"What gave you that impression?" Eric's question came out more surly than he intended.

"IndyCar Medical," Clint replied. "We've been in touch with them since the accident. They said you'd be out for the rest of this year and may not even be ready for the start of next year."

"I'll be ready." Eric's response sounded more defensive than he'd intended. "I mean, I'll be ready for next year. I may even be ready before this season is over."

Clint nodded slowly, his expression softening. "I hope you are, Eric. I really do. And if you're ready before the end of the year, we'll put you back in the car. You have my word."

"Good. That's good, Clint. Thank you." Eric stood, offering his hand once again. "I'm going to Pro Fit now to set up my workout schedule. I'll get back just as soon as I can."

Eric shook Clint's hand and quickly left his boss's office, the weight of the conversation sinking in with every step. Outside, he climbed into his car, his hands trembling slightly as he gripped the wheel. The engine roared to life, and he wiped the sweat from his forehead, feeling the cool air conditioning blow across his face. But even that couldn't shake the panic rising in his gut.

He needed to talk to his manager, Johan Anker, to get this situation straightened out. He dialed Johan's number, waiting for the familiar voice on the other end of the line.

"Eric, how are you feeling?" Johan's voice was chipper, but there was a hint of concern in his Scandinavian accent.

"Not too good at the moment," Eric said. "I just had a visit with Clint. He tells me they've signed Russell Ray for the remainder of the season."

Johan was silent for a moment. "Did you think they wouldn't fill the seat?" His voice was soft and filled with concern.

"No, I mean, I knew they would get someone to replace me, but not for the rest of the year."

"There are barely three months left in the season," Johan said. "You don't think you'll be ready by then, do you?"

"I don't know. Maybe." Eric sighed deeply, the uncertainty creeping back in. "I'm doing good, Johan. I really feel like I could get ready by the end of the year."

"Eric, you broke your neck and fractured your skull. Granted, it could have been worse, but those are still serious injuries that are going to take some time to heal. You can't rush things. That will only make it worse. You need to be patient with yourself."

Eric respected Johan. He was a former driver himself, and he knew what it took to come back from an injury. Eric hated to argue with him, but the urgency of the situation felt like a pressing weight on his chest.

"I can't afford to be patient," Eric's voice tightened. "My contract is up at the end of the year, and if I don't get back in the car, how am I going to find a seat for next season?"

"You let me worry about finding you a seat. Your entire focus needs to be on healing. And once you're healed enough, you can start working out again. But give it time. Just remember, no team is going to consider you until IndyCar Medical says you're ready to get back out on track."

Eric took the phone away from his ear, closing his eyes as Johan's words echoed in his mind. What Johan was saying made perfect sense, but Eric couldn't bring himself to accept it.

"Eric, are you still there?"

"Yeah, I'm here. I'll talk to you later." Eric hung up, feeling the weight of it all settle on him.

The sooner he was physically ready, the sooner IndyCar Medical would have to give their blessing for him to race again. He pulled out of the parking lot and headed for Pro Fit.

The gym was nearly empty, the stillness of the space amplifying his sense of isolation. A lot of his competitors worked out at Pro Fit, and most of the drivers who did preferred to train early in the day. Eric felt the same way. It was better to work out in the morning and have the rest of the day open than to try to shoehorn a workout into the middle of an otherwise busy day.

Justin, Eric's trainer, was in his office, his face hidden behind a book on high performance nutrition. Although Justin was more than a decade out of the Marines, he still wore a military haircut, his hair cropped close on the sides and longer on top. The look gave him an air of discipline, and his no nonsense attitude matched his appearance.

"How are you, Eric?" Justin set the book down, lining it up with the corner of his spotless desk.

"I'm doing well," Eric said. "I'm feeling strong."

"That's great," he said. "And it's good to see you, but what are you doing here?"

Eric was surprised by Justin's blunt question. "I want to schedule some workouts. It's time to get back into shape."

Justin raised an eyebrow, his hands resting flat on the uncluttered desk. "Do you think you're ready for that?"

"I need to be ready. I need to get back into a car."

"Have you started physical therapy yet?"

"I started last week."

"Okay, so once you're done with PT, we can start working out again," Justin said, his voice firm. "But not before."

"But I need to…"

"Hold up a second," Justin said, his tone authoritative. "You were badly injured in a gnarly accident just a month or so ago. You're not nearly ready to start back with your workouts. You understand that, right?"

Eric's frustration simmered, but he knew deep down that Justin was right. He just refused to accept it. "What I understand is that…"

"No, I need you to say that you understand how bad your injuries were, Eric. I need you to say that you understand you're not ready to start working out again."

He sighed audibly, then looked up at Justin. "You're right. I know you're right."

"Do you think you're the first driver to come in here after an accident trying to make their injuries go away by working out? You guys are a different breed, that's for sure. But it doesn't work like that. The body takes time to heal, to repair itself. I know patience isn't your thing, but you need to be patient. Take things one step at a time. Finish PT, then we'll work on getting you back in a car. Sound fair?"

Eric cleared his throat, a reluctant acceptance in his voice. "Yeah, I guess so."

"Great," Justin said. "When you're ready, I'll whip you back into shape. Until then, I don't want to see you in here unless you're bringing lunch for the staff. Understood?"

Eric laughed, a little of the tension lifting off his shoulders. Justin could be a real ball buster, but Eric knew it was for his own good. "Aye, aye, Captain," he said, giving a weak salute.

"Dismissed," Justin said with a smirk. As Eric turned to leave, Justin added, "And work on that salute."

Chapter 13

Eric turned off the light and climbed into bed, the cool sheets brushing against his skin. He pulled the covers up around his neck, the weight of the blankets comforting, but his mind refused to settle. He lay on his back in the dark room, staring at the ceiling. The darkness around him felt confining, but it was the turmoil inside his head that was the heaviest burden.

He thought about his encounter earlier that day with Justin. He knew Justin was right about being patient. If any other driver had asked him for advice following a big shunt like the one he'd experienced, Eric would have told them to take their time, to rest, heal completely, and make sure they were fully ready to race again before climbing back into the car. But for some reason, he couldn't bring himself to follow that same logic. The urgency to get back in the car gnawed at him, the pressure to return to normalcy more overpowering than the reality of his injuries.

His mind began to drift, and with a sudden sharpness, he saw himself in a makeshift office, the cluttered desk in front of him covered with blueprints and invoices, the pressure of unfinished business weighing heavily on him. The office was in a newly constructed home, the air smelling faintly of fresh wood and paint, the trim on the edges of the room unfinished.

A car door slamming outside jolted him, and then footsteps on the hardwood floor echoed, each step growing louder. It was too late for anyone to be coming by for a viewing, but the sound persisted, drawing nearer. He watched, detached, as the figure of a man—his business partner, John Driggins—entered the room, his steps slow but purposeful. Driggins' face was set in a serious expression, his jaw clenched tightly, and Eric felt the undercurrent of tension before a single word was spoken.

"What's going on, John?" Eric's voice low, trying to mask the unease that was creeping up his spine.

Driggins' voice was calm, but there was a tremor of something dark beneath the surface, a barely contained anger seeping through. As he spoke, his voice rose in volume, the control he was trying to maintain slipping away.

"I'll tell you what brought me out tonight," Driggins said. "Earlier today, I found out that you've been sleeping with my wife." The words hit Eric like a kick to the gut, but he held his ground, trying to suppress the instinctual guilt rising in his chest.

"Who told you that?" The knots in Eric's stomach twisted tighter.

"Who told me doesn't matter," Driggins said. "I confronted Bridget about it already and she admitted that the two of you have been seeing each other behind my back for more than a year."

"Bridget said that?" Eric's pulse quickened, and he wondered why Bridget didn't just lie to John. Lying was her strong suit.

"You're damned right she said that." Driggins exhaled sharply, his frustration mounting. He looked around the temporary office, his gaze darting away from Eric's eyes as if he couldn't face him anymore. "I'm going to tell you the same thing I told her." Driggins' voice hardened. "I'm done with the both of you. If you want Bridget, be my guest. The two of you deserve each other. I'm getting the hell out of here. I've taken all of my money out of the business and I'm heading to Arizona."

Eric's heart sank. Without Driggins' money, there was no business. No future. The panic clawed at his chest, but he fought to keep his voice steady.

"This isn't what you think, John," he pleaded. "I can explain."

"Explain what?" Driggins' eyes flashed with disbelief. "Do you honestly think I would believe anything you'd have to say, Ted?"

Ted? Eric's mind jerked to a halt. He assumed that must be the name of whoever's eyes he was looking through; whoever's memory he was experiencing. But who was Ted? His heart pounded in his ears, the confusion deepening. "Come on, John. You've got to listen to me."

"I don't want to waste any more time on this," Driggins said. "My bags are packed, and the car is gassed up. I'm leaving for Arizona tonight. I don't want to see you or my bitch of a wife ever again."

Driggins turned to leave, and in that moment, Eric felt a surge of rage and panic well up inside him. The business, the life he had built, everything was slipping away. His vision blurred as a mix of emotions surged through him, but before he could speak, the scene fractured and snapped back to the present.

Eric jerked upright in bed, his breathing coming in short gasps, as though the weight of the moment he had just witnessed was still pressing down on him. The darkness of the room felt suffocating as he struggled to make sense of what had just happened. The tension in his chest hadn't dissipated. It felt as though the emotions from that scene—rage, betrayal, fear—still clung to him.

His mind went to Dr. Pellegrino. He felt the urge to tell her about his vision—that was what he had come to call the memories that suddenly and unexpectedly would flood his mind. His meeting with her couldn't come soon enough. Maybe talking about it would bring some clarity. Maybe she could help.

CHAPTER 14

D r. Pellegrino sat across from Eric, her posture relaxed yet attentive. The small conference room had an atmosphere of calm efficiency, the round table in the center dominating the space. Soft, sound-deadening material lined the walls, making the room feel insulated, as though the outside world was distant and irrelevant. A thick blackout curtain covered the lone window, preventing light from leaking in. Unlike her office, this room felt sterile and impersonal, the stillness giving the space a clinical feel.

She had her hair pulled back in a loose ponytail, held in place with a soft pink ribbon. The casualness of it—especially the subtle pop of color—made her appear less like the professor he imagined and more like someone with whom he could connect on a personal level. Eric hadn't realized how good looking she was during his first visit. With the ribbon in her hair, she looked more approachable. There was something about the ribbon itself that seemed to draw his attention. It was simple but delicate, and for a brief moment, he found himself wondering if it was the ribbon or Michelle's absence that made him suddenly find the good doctor so attractive.

Dr. Pellegrino explained that the room was set up for recording conversations with her patients. A microphone sat in the center of the table, its sleek dark surface reflecting the soft overhead lights. Two video cameras filmed them from opposing corners, their lenses fixed and unmoving, silently recording the moment.

Eric wasn't sure how he felt about this interview, if "interview" was even the right word. On the one hand, he looked forward to telling Dr.

Pellegrino about the memories crashing through his mind. On the other, attributing them to reincarnation felt too outlandish.

"Let's start with the basics," Dr. Pellegrino said, her voice calm, professional. "How long have you been having these memories?"

"They started after the accident." He leaned forward as he spoke, noticing the faint creases on Dr. Pellegrino's forehead as she made a quick note on her tablet. He couldn't help but admire the focus with which she worked.

"When you say, 'the accident,' are you talking about the one you had while attempting to qualify for the Indianapolis 500?" Dr. Pellegrino's eyes met his, and there was a slight intensity behind them, as though she was studying him just as much as she was studying his memories.

"Yes, that's right."

"Did you sustain any injuries in that accident?"

"I did," he said. "I had a nondisplaced fracture in my neck, and I suffered a fractured skull that required I be placed in a drug-induced coma." Saying the words aloud to someone else made the injuries feel more real, more tangible. He watched Dr. Pellegrino's expression tighten ever so slightly, her face briefly shadowed by concern.

"Did you have any of these memories or anything like them before the accident?" she asked.

"No. Not these. And nothing like them," he said. "I only had my own memories."

"When you say your own memories, tell me what you mean."

"You know, like stuff that happened to me as a kid," he said. "Growing up in Florida, racing karts, moving to Europe. Stuff that actually happened to me." He leaned back in his chair, the old memories of his past life feeling distant, but at least they were his own.

Pellegrino made another note on her tablet before returning her gaze to him. "The memories you're having now, what can you tell me about them?"

The memories had been expanding with each passing day. Gaps were filled in, details added. They seemed to be multiplying, building on one another, each memory flowing into the next like a series of snapshots too fragmented to piece together into one coherent whole. The more he remembered, the less he understood what was happening to him.

"There are a lot of them," he said. "I remember all kinds of things. Like being a construction worker in Chicago, a cattle rancher out west, a butler in London, and a soldier in Canada. That can't all be from one life, can it?" The words felt contrived, as if he was reading from a script instead of speaking about his own experiences.

Dr. Pellegrino smiled, her eyes lighting up with genuine interest. "You could be remembering several different lives. Is there a memory that seems like it's the most recent?"

"That would be the one in Chicago." His mind was already shifting back to the life where he was a construction worker. The familiarity of it washed over him again, more vivid now after the vision he'd had the previous night.

"Tell me about that one." Her tone was inviting, as though she was asking for a story rather than an explanation.

Eric cleared his throat and sat up a little straighter, feeling the weight of the memory as it surfaced. "I started working construction after graduating high school. I liked building things, working with my hands. I did that for several years when this guy, John Driggins, said he wanted us to go into business together, building new homes. It was a pretty sweet deal for me. He had some money, but didn't know much about construction, so I got half the company just to keep doing what I had been doing, building homes." He paused, his mind processing the details. "Whoa, that's a new one."

"What do you mean?"

"I just remembered something I hadn't remembered before." He twisted the cap off the bottle of water and took a quick drink, trying to steady himself. The memory unsettled him, but he wasn't ready to talk about it.

"Are you okay?" Dr. Pellegrino asked, noticing his flushed face. "You seem... affected."

Eric nodded slowly. "Give me a second." He tried to push the new memory aside. If he was really remembering past lives, then this latest revelation was one he didn't want to share. It painted him in a way he wasn't ready to accept, and certainly not to reveal. He wasn't ready for Dr. Pellegrino to judge him or look bad in her eyes. He took another drink of water and composed himself.

Pellegrino waited patiently.

"The business was doing pretty well," Eric continued. "Driggins took care of the money side of things, I took care of the building side. I was at one of the homes we were building. I had an office set up in one of the rooms, and I was sitting at my desk late one night when Driggins came in. He was upset and started screaming at me. He said he knew I was sleeping with his wife and…" He gestured with his hand. "Well, not me, but... you know what I mean. Whoever these memories are from."

"I know what you mean." Her voice was calm and accepting. "Don't get hung up on who it is. If it was you, it's not you anymore."

"Right," Eric said, his voice quieter. He took a moment to gather his thoughts. "Driggins said he knew I was sleeping with his wife and that as far as he was concerned, I could have her. He was done with her and done with the business. He said he had pulled all his money out of our account, and he was going to Arizona."

Pellegrino made more notes. "What happened next?"

Eric shook his head. Sweat trickled down his back as the intensity of the memory deepened. "He left," Eric said. "Went to Arizona. I never heard from him again."

"What about the wife?" Pellegrino asked.

"She never heard from him either."

"I mean, did you end up with Driggins' wife?"

Eric hesitated, his discomfort palpable. "No, I, um…" He shook his head. "When Driggins left with the money, I had to shut down the company. That was 1984. I was broke and I wanted to get out of Chicago, so I rented my uncle's cabin in Wisconsin, near Rhinelander. I lived up there, doing handyman jobs and occasionally working as a fishing guide." His voice quieted. "That is, until I drank myself to death." He looked up at Dr. Pellegrino, his chest tightening with the rawness of the memory. He had been staring down at the table, but now he met her gaze, his emotions raw and exposed.

"That was a sad life." Her voice was quiet, filled with empathy. "Do you need a minute before we get into specifics?"

Tears welled up in Eric's eyes. He wiped them away quickly, trying to regain his composure. "No, I'm okay." He twisted the top off the bottle and took another drink of water, letting the cool liquid soothe his dry throat.

"Do you remember your name in that life?"

Eric nodded, his throat tight. "Ted." And then, almost instinctively, the surname followed. "Humphrey. Ted Humphrey."

"What was the name of the construction company you owned with John Driggins?"

"We called it DH Homes." Eric was surprised by how easily the answer came to him. It felt as though the name had always been there, waiting for the right moment to surface.

"Do you remember the address of your company office?"

Eric hesitated, his brow furrowing as he tried to recall. The sound of the air conditioning hummed softly in the background, a steady presence. "It was on North Rogers Ave, near Peterson. I remember that, but I don't remember the exact address."

"How about your home address?"

"Before I moved to Wisconsin, I lived on Springfield Ave in Lincolnwood."

"Lincolnwood, Illinois?"

"No, it's a neighborhood in Chicago."

"How about your address in Wisconsin?"

"I don't remember my specific address. It was in Rhinelander on Sunset Drive, but back then, we didn't get mail delivered to the house. We had to go into town to pick it up."

"Your uncle that owned the cabin, what was his name?" she asked.

Eric thought for a moment. "Emil Humphrey."

"Do you remember the name of Driggins' wife?"

Eric hesitated. "Are all of these specifics really that important?"

"Anything that I can check into to confirm your memories. Driggins' wife's name isn't all that important to my research other than for me to have something specific to investigate."

"Bridget," Eric said, after a brief pause.

"What?"

"Driggins' wife. Her name was Bridget."

Pellegrino wrote down the information. "Did you ever try to find Driggins after he moved to Arizona?"

"No. Why would I do that?" Eric asked. His response was more defensive than he had intended.

"I don't know," she said. "Maybe to apologize or try to mend fences."

Eric shook his head. "No."

"Do you remember how you died?"

Eric shifted in his chair, uncomfortable with the memories that flooded in. "I remember drinking a lot after moving up to Wisconsin. I used to drink at a bar called Henkel's or Henkie's. Something like that. It was close to the cabin. But once I got kicked out of there, I drank mostly at home. I remember being sick, and getting sicker, but instead of doing anything about it, I just kept drinking. One day, I started drinking early. Having beer for breakfast wasn't all that unusual. But it was winter, and I got the bright idea to head out onto the lake to do some ice fishing. Unfortunately, the ice was thin. It broke, and I fell in. I remember, I didn't even fight it. I just sank into the darkness of the water and I drowned."

"Do you remember the date?"

Eric looked up at the ceiling, then shook his head. "No. I remember there was snow on the ground and the lake had ice on it, so it must have been winter, but I don't remember the exact date."

"Can you remember anything else?"

Eric shifted again in his chair, the memories still flooding in, but he wanted to process them before telling her about them. "No, that's it for that life."

"Okay." Pellegrino exhaled. "Let's move on to the next one."

CHAPTER 15

Not ready to recount another life to Dr. Pellegrino, Eric excused himself to go to the bathroom to collect his thoughts. The bathroom was small, its dim light cast a faint golden glow over the sink and mirror. Eric splashed water on his face, watching as droplets ran down his reflection, distorting the haunted expression staring back at him. The faint aroma of lavender from the soft soap on the counter filled the air as he gripped the edge of the sink, trying to calm the whirlwind churning up inside him.

He had not expected to get upset about his memories, but he had. Memories of his life as Ted Humphrey had given him chills, crawling under his skin and settling over him like a cold fog. Ever since the accident, more and more memories had filled his head. His visions were happening more frequently, adding depth and unsettling details to his recollections. But now, talking about it, answering Dr. Pellegrino's questions, the floodgates had opened. The tide of memories threatened to overwhelm him, each wave bringing not only vivid images but also emotions, grief, fear, despair.

He feared what else might surface as they continued to talk. The thought of walking out of the office flashed briefly in his mind, but it felt cowardly. Better to rip the bandage off all at once than to allow the memories to trickle in, day after day after day. Eric dried his face with a paper towel, the texture of the paper rough against his skin, and returned to the conference room. He paused at the door, taking one last deep breath before returning to the fray.

Back at the table with Dr. Pellegrino, he was willing, if not ready, to move on to a different set of memories. The stark whiteness of the interview room walls seemed to reinforce his unease. He hoped moving on would get his mind off the sad, tragic life of Ted Humphrey.

"Can you tell which of your memories came right before your time in Chicago?" Dr. Pellegrino asked.

Eric nodded. "That would be my life in Canada."

"What can you tell me about that life?"

"Honestly, I don't have a lot of memories from that life," he said. "My name was Tim Holt. I was born and raised in Saguenay, Quebec, northeast of Montreal. I had a sister named Florence who was more of a mother to me than a sister. I was the youngest in the family, and my birth wasn't planned. My parents were older. Florence ended up taking care of me most of the time."

"You were an oopsie baby," Pellegrino said, her lips quirking into a brief smile.

"A what?"

Dr Pellegrino chuckled. "That's what my mother called an unplanned pregnancy. An oopsie baby."

Eric nodded his head slowly, considering her words. "Yeah, I guess I was an oopsie baby."

"I'm sorry, I shouldn't have interrupted," she said, trying to regain her professional composure. "Please, go on."

He sighed and tried to assemble his memories of life in Canada into a coherent story. He took a deep breath, then exhaled slowly.

"I don't remember much about my parents," he said, his voice tinged with regret. "They weren't around a lot. Florence, my sister, was the one constant in my life. I had a cousin who hung out at our house. His name was Richard, but everyone called him Dickie. He was a couple years older than me and was mean. He used to bully me all the time. I remember him spending a lot of time in the woods, shooting squirrels and neighborhood cats."

"He killed our dog." Eric's face darkened. "Her name was Ranger. We found her hanging from a tree in the backyard. Dickie had wrapped a rope around her neck and hung her from a branch. We couldn't prove it was Dickie, but Florence and I knew he'd done it."

"That's horrible."

Eric nodded, his gaze distant. "Florence tried to protect me from Dickie. He was sadistic. Maybe there was something mentally wrong with him. You know, like he was mentally ill. But I guess we didn't know much about that back then. Anyway, Florence did her best, but she couldn't look out for me twenty-four hours a day. I wanted to avoid Dickie so bad that, as soon as I was old enough, I joined the military. That got me away from Dickie but landed me in the middle of World War II."

Dr. Pellegrino made a quick note, her pen scratching against the tablet. "Can you tell me about your time in the military?"

"There's not much to tell." He shook his head. "I joined the Army and was part of the Canadian D-Day landing. I died in the Netherlands on April 4, 1945." Eric looked up at the ceiling as if searching for something. He took a deep breath and let it out slowly. "I wasn't shot. I drowned in this life too, just a few yards from the landing craft. I never made it to the beach."

Eric expected the revelation about his death to be upsetting, but it wasn't, at least not as upsetting as recounting his death when he was Ted. "It feels weird to be so matter of fact about what is supposedly my own death."

Pellegrino smiled gently and nodded, jotting down another note. Her expression was calm, though her eyes held a flicker of something— empathy, perhaps, or a deep curiosity. "How about the life before your life in Canada?"

"I lived in London. I was a butler." Eric's eyes suddenly widened in surprise. "I was black." The words hung in the air, laden with the weight of an epiphany.

Pellegrino's questions continued, familiar but methodical, yet Eric found his memories of that life more fragmented, as if time had worn away the edges of his past. And yet, the life unfolded with an eerie vividness, the memories threading through his mind like a patchwork quilt, each fragment hinting at a larger, fuller, but no less mysterious, whole.

Dr. Pellegrino leaned forward slightly, her expression contemplative. "Do you remember who employed you as a butler or any other details about that life?"

Eric leaned back in his chair, his fingers tapping lightly on the table. "Yes. My employer's name was Lord Daniel Timpson. He was…not a kind man." Eric's tone grew sharper, his words edged with the bitterness of old wounds. "He liked to belittle me, and when he drank, he'd hit me with his cane. I suppose it was common back then, but it doesn't make it any easier to remember."

"What happened to you during that life?" Pellegrino asked.

"I died of tuberculosis," Eric said flatly. "Lord Timpson sent me to a sanitarium when I got sick. I never saw him again."

Dr. Pellegrino nodded thoughtfully, her pen darting across the tablet as Eric's memories continued to unfold. The fragments of Eric's past lives seemed to intertwine, weaving a complex tapestry of pain, resilience, and unanswered questions.

"Is there anything else?"

Eric shook his head. "I'm sorry, the memories of that life are kind of vague."

She nodded. "The further back you go, the less you'll remember, I suppose, which makes sense."

"Except, I remember a lot about the life I had before I was a butler in London."

"Tell me about that life."

Eric shifted in his chair. "I was born in 1812 near the Mississippi River, in the northern part of the Illinois Territory. My family owned a small farm where we had cattle and pigs and chickens. I couldn't wait to get out on my own. My parents were strict Congregationalists, believing that the Bible was the one true word of God. Sunday church services sometimes went on for hours. But there were other things I wanted to do, so as soon as I was old enough, I left home and made my way out west."

Eric closed his eyes. "I ended up in what was called the Nebraska Territory. For a while, it was called the Jefferson Territory, but shortly before I died, it became the State of Colorado." Eric cleared his throat and tried to mentally form his memories into a story that made sense.

"I met a man named E.J. Barrett, a cattle rancher and businessman. He was looking for someone to help him with his cattle and I was looking for a job. He became like a second father to me. He took me under his wing and taught me how to raise cattle on the short grass prairies and foothills. And he introduced me to his daughter, Rachel."

"Do you remember your name?" she asked. "Were you married or did you have children?"

"My name was Cole Keillor, and I married Rachel." A smile spread across his face, remembering his wife from that lifetime.

"Is there more?"

Eric nodded. "I became more like a partner than an employee to E.J.," he said. "Rachel and I fell in love. We were married right there on the ranch. E.J. and I built a home—a small cabin—for Rachel and me." Eric's demeanor suddenly changed. His smile faded and his expression became serious, his voice quiet. "Rachel died a couple of years after we were married. She was pregnant. I lost her and the baby. I lived out my days on the ranch. After E.J. died, it was just me and a few hired hands. I never got over losing Rachel."

Eric stared at his hands lying flat on the table, the memory of Rachel weighing heavy on his mind. While his death during World War II seemed matter of fact, he genuinely felt Rachel's loss. He fought back tears. When he finally looked up, Pellegrino was wiping tears from her eyes.

She took a deep breath, trying to control her emotions. "Can you remember anything else from that life?"

"I remember I died in 1878," he said. "I was sixty-six years old. I was gray, weathered, and ready to die. Life with Rachel had been wonderful, but life after Rachel seemed to drag on."

Pellegrino made some notes.

"Seems weird that I remember so much from that life even though it happened before my life in London, doesn't it?" he asked.

"It's a little strange, I suppose, but it seems that your connection to Rachel made that life somehow more profound than your lives in London or Canada. Maybe even more profound than the one in Chicago."

Eric nodded, rubbing his hands on the tabletop.

"Do you remember other lives?" she asked.

"Not really. Just bits and pieces," he said. "Before my life with Rachel, I was a stonemason in Ireland. Before that, I was in England, I think, but I don't remember much about either of those lives."

"That's okay. For our purposes, we want to investigate memories that you have that are detailed and where documentation exists to potentially confirm your memories. The next step for me is to look into everything you've told me to see if I can support or reject your memories."

"You said during our last meeting that you don't believe in reincarnation," Eric said. "If you don't believe, why do you do this kind of work?"

Pellegrino put her tablet on the table and focused her attention on Eric. "To say I don't believe is inaccurate," she said. "I'm agnostic. I can't prove reincarnation is real or that it's not real. No one can. So, I just document my findings and hope that it helps us understand what happens when we die. I can tell you, I've investigated many cases where reincarnation is the most reasonable, logical answer."

"Why don't I hear much about reincarnation?" he asked. "Before this all happened, I barely ever heard anything about it."

"Many of the interviews I've conducted have been outside the United States, mostly in India and Lebanon," she said. "In the United States, we are conditioned to disbelieve in reincarnation. But in India and Lebanon, as well as a few other places, the culture is much more accepting. Reincarnation is part of the religious beliefs there, primarily Hindu and the Druze sect of Islam. The problem is that most of the people with memories of past lives are children. They often have trouble expressing what it is they remember, and there's seldom adequate documentation to confirm many of the claims being made. Working with you is a rare opportunity to interview someone who can articulate their memories in a detailed enough fashion for those memories to be investigated thoroughly."

Eric sighed. "I still have trouble accepting that what I'm experiencing are memories of my past lives."

"Why are you skeptical?"

"There are a lot of reasons," he said. "For instance, don't you think it's strange that I'm always reborn in an English-speaking country, I'm always straight, and with one exception, I'm always white. And in each life, I'm male."

Pellegrino pursed her lips and nodded her head. "I understand your skepticism," she said. "Let's think it through. It's not as unusual as you might think that you were reborn in English-speaking countries. In fact, the research shows that most people we have spoken to with past life memories are reborn in the same country, often in or near the same village. You might expect your lives to be spread out all over the world, but the research indicates it is more common to be reborn near the same location, sometimes over and over again."

Eric nodded, indicating he was following her, but this was all new information to him.

"It's also not unusual that in each of the past lives you are remembering, you were straight," she said. "It's estimated that about ninety percent of people on earth are heterosexual. So, the fact that you were always straight isn't that surprising. And remember, being gay is more accepted now than it has been at any time in our history, so it's possible you were gay or had gay tendencies in past lives but didn't recognize what you were feeling due to cultural norms."

"You're saying I could have been gay but didn't know it?" he asked.

Pellegrino laughed. "That's a little more simplistic than what I'm saying, but it's close." She leaned forward in her seat. "I have a theory. I can't prove it, just like I can't prove that reincarnation is real. But I have a theory that some—maybe most—gay men and lesbian women have the gender attraction they have because they were the opposite gender in a previous life."

"There is a certain logic to that," Eric said. "Why do you think I'm always reborn white?"

"Not always. Don't forget about your time in London as a butler. But I understand what you're asking. It might be related to where you were reborn. If the majority of the people are white, then it's more likely that you'd be reborn as a white person. Rather than being surprised that you were almost always white, maybe you should be more surprised that you were reborn as a black man in an overwhelmingly white England."

"What about always being a man?"

"I don't have an easy answer for you on that one. There's some research that indicates that we choose the body we're going to be born into. For some reason, maybe you've always chosen a male body, although I can't explain why that might be.

"I guess there's a lot I don't know," he said. "So, from what I've told you, you think all these memories I'm having are proof of reincarnation?"

She shook her head. "It's too soon to say that. I need to complete my investigation before I can say. And even then, I won't be able to say it's definitely reincarnation."

"If it's not, what else could it be?"

"There's a phenomenon called paramnesia," she said. "I've run into it before in India. It's a condition where an interview subject remembers things that never happened. They truly believe it happened, but the investigation into it reveals that it didn't."

Eric tilted his head. "I don't understand."

"I'll give you an easy example," she said. "When I was a child, my mum cut her hand with a knife. She was chopping vegetables. I went running through the kitchen and ran into her, causing her to cut herself. I felt guilty about it for years. I mentioned it to her long after it happened, and she had no idea what I was talking about. 'You didn't run into me,' she said. 'You were in school when that happened.' I can't tell you why

I have that memory, but that's the type of thing I'm talking about. It's a sincerely held memory of something that never happened."

"And you think that might be what I'm experiencing?"

"It's too soon to tell," she said. "You have so many memories and most of them are so detailed, paramnesia wouldn't seem to fit. But it will take some time to figure that out. Keep an open mind and I'll let you know what happens as I investigate further." She stood, signaling the end of the session.

Eric stood as well, feeling the weight of the discussion but also a strange lightness at having shared so much. "Thank you, Dr. Pellegrino," he said, his voice subdued.

She smiled warmly. "It's probably best if you just call me Carly from now on."

Eric returned the smile, a small flicker of hope breaking through the haze of his confusion. "Okay, Thanks, Carly."

Chapter 16

Eric was in the kitchen eating a bowl of cereal when the back door opened and Michelle walked in. She had her blond hair pulled back and wore sunglasses. She took the glasses off once she was in the house, the faint indentation of the frames still visible on the bridge of her nose.

"Welcome home." Eric set the spoon down in his nearly empty bowl. "How was your trip?"

Michelle had been working at the race in Portland, doing PR work for one of the teams. Her shoulders relaxed slightly as she leaned against the counter. "It was good," she said. "Everyone was asking about you. Did you watch the race?"

"I did," Eric said, a lack of enthusiasm evident in his voice.

"And?"

"It was a good race," he said. "I wish I would have been there."

Michelle put her hands on her hips and stared at him, her blue eyes narrowing slightly. "What?" he asked, sensing her disapproval before she spoke.

"You know what." Her tone carried a hint of exasperation. "Aren't you going to say anything about Russell finishing on the podium?"

"There's nothing to say." Eric shrugged. "He's a good driver in a good car, backed up by a good team."

"That's it?" she asked, her voice rising slightly.

Eric took the last bite of his cereal, and walked the bowl to the sink, the ceramic clinking lightly as he set it down. "I don't know what you want me to say, Michelle. Russell is in my seat, and he finished on the podium. I wish I was in the car, but I'm not. There's not much else to say."

Michelle sighed, the sound heavy with unspoken frustration. She moved to where Eric had been sitting. Eric stood at the sink, his back to her.

"Did you meet with that fake doctor yet?" she asked.

Eric laughed lightly and turned around, leaning against the counter. "She's not a fake doctor. She's a PhD. And yes, I met with her."

"Does she still think that you're remembering past lives?"

"That's not how it works. She doesn't make a diagnosis…"

"You mean like a real doctor?" Michelle asked. There was a sharpness to her voice.

Eric sighed, turning to face her. "I told her what I was remembering. She asked a bunch of questions, and now she's going to look into what I told her. She wants to see if she can confirm anything that I'm remembering."

"How does she do that?" Michelle asked. "Does she use a crystal ball?"

Eric shook his head, making no attempt to hide his frustration. "She looks for documentation like birth certificates, driver's licenses, property records, obituaries, things like that. And even after she does her investigation, she still doesn't say whether I'm remembering past lives. She just presents the evidence, and it's up to me to decide what I believe."

"She sounds like a con artist who's trying to defraud you."

"Defraud me how?" Eric asked, his tone clipped. "I'm just telling her what I remember."

"Think about it, Eric. She has an Italian name, speaks with an English accent, and lives in Indiana. Who does that?"

Eric wasn't sure what point Michelle was trying to make. He tilted his head slightly. "How about Dario Franchitti?"

"What are you talking about?"

"Dario Franchitti has an Italian name, speaks with a Scottish accent, and lives in Indiana," he said. "Or how about Scott Dixon? He's from New Zealand, has a Kiwi accent, and splits his time between England and here. Do you think they're frauds?"

Michelle stood abruptly, the chair scraping against the floor. She walked to the door, her movements quick and deliberate. "Of course they're not frauds. But you just wait," she said, pointing at Eric. "This will eventually cost you. Maybe not money, but somehow." She pushed the door open and stepped through, letting it slam shut behind her.

Later that night, Eric was at the stove when Michelle walked through the back door into the kitchen. He glanced over his shoulder, surprised to see her smiling. It had been several hours since she stormed out, and for most of the day, he wasn't sure she'd come back for their planned dinner.

"Hi." Her tone was light, almost playful.

"Hi," he said. "Are you still mad at me?"

Michelle walked up behind him as he stirred the red sauce simmering in the pot, the aroma of tomatoes and herbs filling the kitchen. She wrapped her arms around his waist, resting her chin on his shoulder. "I'm sorry, babe. I wasn't mad. I was just worried about you."

Eric stopped stirring the sauce and turned around to face her. He placed his hands gently on her hips and kissed her. "Really?" he asked. "Because it seemed like you were mad."

"Oh, let's just forget about it and enjoy our evening together."

"That sounds good to me." He turned back toward the stove. "Dinner should be ready in a few minutes."

"Great!" she said. "I'm going to have a glass of wine and watch you cook. I think it's sexy."

"What is?" he asked. "The wine or me cooking?"

Michelle laughed as she poured herself a glass of white wine from a bottle she had taken out of the refrigerator. "You cooking," she said. "But the wine doesn't hurt."

"If you think me cooking is sexy, you should see me do laundry."

She laughed again, the sound filling the kitchen and softening the tension from earlier. She sat at the kitchen table, her glass of wine in hand. "There's just one more thing I want to say about that doctor of yours."

Eric knew Michelle well enough to know that she wasn't capable of letting something go that she felt strongly about. And she felt strongly about a lot of things.

"You know I'm just looking out for your own good, right?" she asked.

Eric nodded, waiting for her to finish her thought.

"I just don't want to see anyone take advantage of you."

"I don't see any way Dr. Pellegrino is going to take advantage of me."

"I know you don't." Michelle sighed and calmed her voice. She had to share a harsh truth with Eric, and she wanted to make sure he heard her. "It's because you're so trusting, and you expect that everyone has the same motivations as you. But they don't, babe. Some people are out to take advantage of trusting souls like yourself."

There was no way for him to win an argument on this subject with Michelle, so he remained quiet.

"Do me a favor," Michelle said. "Don't go back to see her, okay? It's not in your best interest, and there's nothing she can do to help you. Can you do that for me?"

Eric pursed his lips and nodded. "I'm done interviewing with her, Michelle."

"Good." She walked over to where he stood in front of the stove and kissed him gently on the lips. "That's good. Now let's forget about all of that so you can feed me." She kissed him again.

CHAPTER 17

The previous night with Michelle made him feel guilty. He felt like being with her was somehow a betrayal of Rachel, an incongruous feeling he couldn't fully explain. How was he betraying Rachel, a woman he only knew through these crazy memories he was having?

But there was a gravity to his memory of her. It was deep and profound. He felt a connection to this woman from his visions unlike anything he had previously felt in his life.

He closed his eyes and saw Rachel on the porch of their cabin as he rode in from tending cattle. The way the sun played off her strawberry blond hair made him yearn to touch her. He remembered hitching his horse and walking up to her on the porch. She smiled, her white teeth contrasting with her sun-bronzed skin.

"Howdy, cowboy," she said.

"Howdy, yourself." He reached for her, and she fell into his arms. They embraced and she turned her face up to his, preparing for his kiss. He leaned down and she parted her lips…

"I need to take off," Michelle said. "I have work to do."

Michelle wore the same clothes she had worn the previous night, yet she looked completely put together. Her hair was done, and her makeup was perfect. How could she always look so ready to take on the world?

Eric stood and they exchanged a quick kiss. "Have a great day."

Michelle gave a slight wave as she went through the front door. "Ciao."

He fell heavily onto the couch and tried to understand this thing he was feeling. He had been with Michelle for more than a year. And during that time, he had not so much as kissed another woman.

He looked up at the ceiling and put his hands over his face. It was rare for him to act on emotion rather than logic, but that's what he was doing in this case.

He rubbed his face, then closed his eyes. What if Michelle was right and the memories that were coursing through his head were not from his past lives? Then where did that leave him? He could accept that the memories had nothing to do with reincarnation. Hell, he wasn't even sure he believed in such a thing. When he was with Dr. Pellegrino—Carly—he felt like it could be true that he lived other lives before. When he was away from her and thought about it, it just didn't seem possible, despite his visions. But if it wasn't reincarnation, then where did these memories come from? He had no other answer.

He took a deep breath and let it out slowly. Okay, what if Michelle was wrong and what he was experiencing were past life memories? That meant that he had once been Ted Humphrey, Tim Holt, Cornelius Hopper, Cole Keillor, and others whose names he couldn't remember.

He hadn't thought about it previously, but each of his alleged past lives seemed to line up chronologically. There didn't appear to be any overlap in the timeline. Was that true?

He jumped up off the couch and went to the extra bedroom that served as his home office. He grabbed a pad of paper and a pen, then returned to the living room. He wrote down the names of each of the people whose memories were in his head, then thought about what he knew about them.

He remembered that Ted Humphrey was born in 1950 and died in 1991. Next was Tim Holt. Tim died in 1945, but when was he born? It took a second to remember, then Eric wrote "1926" on the pad of paper next to Tim's name.

He didn't have as many memories of Hopper as he did some of his other supposed past lives. Memories of his time in London were foggy in his mind, but he did remember that Hopper was born in 1880 and died in 1922. Just 42 years old.

He had a longer life when he was Cole. He was born in 1812 and died sixty-six years later in 1878. He wrote his age at death next to each name on the pad of paper and stared at it for a moment. He hadn't lived very long when he was Hopper, Tim, or Ted, dying young in all those lifetimes. Cole's life was longer, which could be why he remembered that life better than his lives as Hopper or Tim, and as well as his most recent past life as Ted.

Depending on the life, there were somewhere between two and five years between the death of one of the people he was remembering and the birth of the next one. Hell, even between when Ted died and Eric was born, there was four years. To Eric's mind, that was a trend, a pattern that was hard to ignore.

He stared at the pad of paper and wrote down Rachel's name next to Cole's, then circled it. Eric's eyes narrowed as he stared at the paper in front of him. Not only had Cole not remarried after Rachel's death, but Hopper, Tim, and Ted never married. Three consecutive lives and none of them ever married. That had to be more than a coincidence.

Now, in this lifetime, he and Michelle had talked about the possibility of getting married. Although neither of them was in a rush, they had both accepted that they would eventually become husband and wife. But now, being with Michelle made him feel guilty and uncomfortable, like he was doing something he shouldn't be doing. Of course, that wasn't fair to Michelle. She hadn't done anything to make him feel that way. But he couldn't deny that he was feeling guilty.

His logic was betraying him. He couldn't bring himself to accept that his memories were from lives he had lived in the past, but he also couldn't come up with an alternative explanation. He let out a loud, guttural groan.

Chapter 18

Dr. Ferris had Eric tilt his neck to the left and then to the right. The exam room was quiet except for the faint, indecipherable murmur of voices in the hallway. "Try to touch your ear to your shoulder," Dr. Ferris said.

Eric's neck felt much more limber than it had during his last visit, but he couldn't touch his ear to his shoulder. He let out a frustrated sigh, the corners of his mouth tightening as he straightened up.

"Don't worry about that," Dr. Ferris said, a reassuring tone to his voice. "You're doing fine. Very few people can touch their ear to their shoulder without cheating. I'm pleased with the progress you've made. How is physical therapy going?"

"It's been good," Eric said. "I only have a few more sessions left. But I'm worried I've lost a lot of strength in my neck. I need to start working out again."

Dr. Ferris shook his head, his expression a mixture of understanding and caution. "It's still too soon for you to do that, Eric. One step at a time."

Eric frowned. "When can I start working out?"

Dr. Ferris finished typing notes into the computer that sat on the desk in the corner, the rhythmic clicking of the keys punctuating the silence. He then turned his full attention to Eric, his tone shifting to measured authority. "You can start working out once you're completely done with PT. But let me warn you, you don't want to go too hard at first. If you're not patient, you could reinjure yourself and set your recovery back weeks, maybe even months."

"I'll be patient," Eric said. "But let me ask you something. Do you think I'll be able to get back into a race car this year?"

Dr. Ferris narrowed his eyes slightly, studying Eric for a moment. "Aren't there only two races left in the season?"

Eric nodded, his jaw tightening.

Dr. Ferris chuckled softly, his arms crossing as he leaned against the exam table. "It doesn't sound like you're being very patient."

"I'm just asking." Eric shrugged and a faint, disarming smile spread across his face.

Dr. Ferris sighed, his smile fading as he grew more serious. "Let me give you a more realistic expectation," he said. "Finish up your PT sessions. Don't rush through them. Take them seriously and do what the therapist says. That will get you ready to go back into the gym. Once you're there, take it easy. Go slow. Be patient. You need to build up your strength and flexibility. Forget about getting into a car this season. There just isn't enough time. Set your sights on getting cleared by IndyCar Medical, then be ready for the start of next season. That's a more realistic plan."

Eric nodded slowly, his gaze dropping to the floor. He didn't like what Dr. Ferris was saying, although he knew it made sense. All along, he had hoped he could get back into a car before the end of the season, but in the back of his mind, he knew it was unlikely.

"Thanks, Doc," Eric said, standing and extending a hand. "I'll focus on next year."

Dr. Ferris shook his hand firmly, his expression one of encouragement. "You're doing great, Eric. Stick to the plan. You'll get there."

Outside, the clear summer air surrounded Eric. The humidity that plagued so many Indianapolis summer days had taken a hiatus, at least for a few days. Eric breathed in the air, allowing it to clear his head.

Next season. The words felt heavy in his mind, a reminder of how far he still had to go. But he couldn't deny that Dr. Ferris was right. Patience would have to be his most important tool. He took a deep breath, the fresh air invigorating him, then exhaled slowly. Now, if he could just figure out where to find some patience.

CHAPTER 19

Eric had to admit, he felt nervous. The warm September air in Nashville carried the scent of motor oil and roasted peanuts, an oddly comforting combination that reminded him of better times at the track. He hadn't been to a race since the accident, and he wasn't sure what to expect. He was looking forward to seeing everyone, but he mostly wanted to talk to Clint about signing a new contract for the following year. The sooner he signed a contract, the more he could relax and concentrate on getting into shape for the next season.

He hadn't said anything to Michelle about being nervous, but she knew. Her ability to read him was uncanny. She took his hand as they walked through the paddock, the distant roar of engines rumbling in the background. "Are you okay?"

"Sure. Everything's fine." His voice carried a slight tone of apprehension. His fingers tightened around hers, seeking reassurance.

She looked at him with a knowing smile. "You'll be fine." She gave his hand a gentle squeeze. "I'm sure Clint will be happy to see you."

He smiled back and nodded, though the knot in his stomach refused to loosen.

Michelle stopped walking and turned toward him, her blond hair catching the sunlight. "I have to go see Tim Buford about doing some work for his team this off-season. Text me when you're done talking to Clint, okay?"

Eric agreed, and Michelle was off. She moved with purpose, her high heels clicking against the concrete as she disappeared into the crowd of team personnel and fans.

Sometimes, Eric wished he could be as focused and single-minded as Michelle. She never let anything get in the way of her work. It wasn't that he wasn't serious about his career. There was nothing he would rather be doing with his life than driving a race car. But there was something about Michelle's commitment to her work that he found both inspiring and a little off-putting. At times, it seemed all-consuming. Even after a little more than a year together, he knew in his heart of hearts that if she ever had to choose between him and her career, her career would win out. That thought cast a shadow over their relationship.

He had managed to put his feelings of guilt and betrayal away in recent weeks. He had packed up those feelings and locked them in a mental drawer. Whether he could keep them there indefinitely was another question.

He shook his head. It was probably best not to think too much about that. He wanted to be clear-eyed and focused for his talk with Clint.

When he got to the garage, he saw Clint outside, talking to a couple of men Eric didn't recognize. As he approached, the men walked away, and Clint turned to see him.

"Eric, how are you?" Clint asked, his voice warm and his expression genuine. He seemed sincerely happy to see Eric.

"I'm doing great, boss," Eric said. "How are things with you?"

"Can't complain," Clint said, a small smile playing at his lips. "The weekend's going well so far. What brings you to the track?"

"I was hoping to talk to you for a few minutes," Eric said, his tone measured.

Clint looked around the garage area, then nodded. "Let's head over to hospitality. We can talk there."

They walked together to the team's hospitality tent, exchanging small talk. Eric struggled to say anything intelligent, his mind focused on his contract.

"Have you been able to go out to see the sights since you've been in Nashville?" Clint asked.

"No, we just got into town last night, then came out to the track first thing this morning."

"We were down on Lower Broad last night," Clint said. "Bars and restaurants for as far as the eye can see. It was a good time. You should check it out while you're in town."

"Maybe tonight," Eric said. "I'll have to see if Michelle is up for it."

When they got to the team's hospitality tent, Clint motioned to a table away from everyone else. "We can talk over there. Do you want a soda or coffee or anything?"

"No thanks. I'm fine."

They sat at a small round wooden table, Eric's back to the tent wall. Clint sat in a chair facing Eric. "There's something I want to tell you, Eric." Clint leaned forward in his chair, crossing his arms on the table.

Eric sat back in his chair, waiting to hear what Clint had to say before he made his pitch.

"I wanted to let you know that after the race, I'm going to announce that we've signed Russell for next season. I was going to call Johan to let him know, but since you're here, I want to tell you in person."

Eric felt his throat fall into his stomach. He scratched the back of his head, then smoothed the hair down. "I was hoping we could talk before you made any decisions."

Clint nodded, his expression tinged with regret. "I understand. But with you not being cleared by IndyCar Medical yet, we had to make a move. We didn't want to lose out on Russell just to find out that your recovery has been delayed. I'm sorry, Eric. I hope you understand."

Eric felt a panic shoot through him. He wanted to change Clint's mind, but it appeared to be a done deal. There was nothing he could say to alter the situation.

Eric sighed. "Thanks for letting me know, Clint. I appreciate your honesty."

"I need to get back to the garage." Clint stood and offered his hand. "Good luck, Eric. I'm sure you'll land on your feet."

Eric shook Clint's hand, then Clint walked quickly out of the tent. Eric sat down heavily and let out a grunt. Now he was well and truly unemployed, and he wasn't sure what he was going to do about it.

He pulled his cell phone from his pocket and dialed Johan's number. Johan answered on the second ring.

"Hey, Eric. What's up?"

Eric told Johan about his conversation with Clint. "The worst part was that I barely said anything. I think I was in shock. I still am."

"I was afraid this might happen," Johan said. "I guess we shouldn't be too surprised. I've spoken with a couple of other teams, but just preliminary talks. You let me worry about finding your next contract. You concentrate on getting healthy. It will be easier to pin down a seat once you're cleared by IndyCar Medical."

"I meet with Medical week after next," he said. "I'll be ready."

"That's good. Let me get busy. I'll find you a great ride, Eric. Don't worry about it."

When they hung up, Eric felt slightly better than he had before the call. He knew his manager would do everything in his power to find a ride for him. Now, he just needed to get ready to pass the IndyCar physical.

He texted Michelle and told her she should meet him at the Catalyst Racing hospitality tent when she finished. He was prepared for a long wait, but Michelle showed up just ten minutes later.

"That was quick," he said.

Michelle was all smiles. "Everything went great," she said. "They want to hire me to fill in for their usual PR person. She's going to be on maternity leave for a few months, so I have a contract for most of the off-season."

"That's great," he said. "Congratulations."

"I still have to find a team to represent next season, but at least the next few months are covered. How did your talk go with Clint?"

"Oh, he only had time to say hi. We're going to talk next week, once things slow down." Eric felt bad lying to Michelle. She would find out the truth eventually, but he just didn't want to spend the rest of the day listening to her drone on about what he should have done differently or what he should do now. He appreciated her support and knew her advice would come from a place of love and concern, but he just couldn't deal with her certainty and self-righteousness right now.

"Oh, too bad. Should we go out and walk the paddock?" she asked.

"Actually, I'm not feeling great," he said. "I'd like to go back to the hotel."

CHAPTER 20

When Eric arrived at Carly's office, she greeted him at the door, her face lighting up with an excited smile. "I found so much good stuff. I can't wait to tell you about it." She practically vibrated with energy.

Her enthusiasm was infectious, and Eric couldn't help but smile as he followed her down the hallway. He took a seat on the same couch he had sat on with Michelle during his previous visit. The room was filled with the faint scent of ginger and vanilla, reminding him of that first visit.

There was something different about Carly today. She was more upbeat and energized than Eric had ever seen her, almost as if the discoveries she had made had infused her with a new vitality. Her eyes sparkled as she arranged a folder and her tablet on her desk. Whatever she had uncovered about his supposed previous lives seemed to be fueling her passion for her work, and Eric found it endearing.

"Let's start with your life as Ted Humphrey," she said, flipping open the folder. "I found a birth certificate for a Theodore Roosevelt Humphrey, born April 18, 1950, in Chicago. I also found a death certificate for you dated December 14, 1991, from Wisconsin."

Eric's eyebrows shot up in mock disbelief. "I never thought I'd hear someone tell me they found a death certificate for me." He chuckled, and Carly joined in, her laughter light and genuine.

"I should clarify—the death certificate was for Ted Humphrey," she said, clearing her throat and smiling. "I also found a birth certificate and an Illinois driver's license for John Anthony Driggins, but I couldn't find a death certificate in either Arizona or Illinois, and I couldn't find a new driver's license for him in Arizona either. I checked the obituaries in both places too but came up empty. He's either still alive out there somewhere, which is possible, or I just haven't looked in the right place yet. Are you sure he went to Arizona when he left Chicago?"

Eric shifted uncomfortably. "Yeah, as far as I know. I never saw him again after he left, so he could have gone anywhere."

"I'll have to do some more digging," she said, jotting a note on her tablet. "I found a marriage certificate for John and Bridget Driggins, which indicated that Bridget's maiden name was Pritchard. That led me to her birth certificate, as well as another marriage license from 1992 where she married someone named Gregory Faulkner. Does that name ring a bell?"

"No, I've never heard of him," he said.

"Anyway, they live in Bloomington, Illinois, now."

Eric's breath caught in his throat. "Bridget is still alive?"

"Yes, she's 79 years old now. I'm planning on having a chat with her next week."

A wave of unease washed over Eric. "Why would you do that?"

"Just more confirmation," Carly said. "I want to find out if she had an affair with Ted Humphrey while she was married to John Driggins, and I want to see if she ever spoke to Driggins after he left Chicago."

Eric's face darkened, a sour look spreading across it.

"Is there a problem?" Carly asked, tilting her head slightly.

"No," he said, leaning back and crossing his arms. "What else did you find?"

Carly flipped through the folder on her lap. "I found the incorporation papers for DH Homes with an address on Rogers Avenue in Chicago, just like you said. It listed John Anthony Driggins and Theodore Roosevelt Humphrey as the lone owners and shareholders."

She shuffled through more papers until she found what she was looking for. "Property records show that Theodore Roosevelt Humphrey owned a home on Springfield Avenue in Chicago that was sold in 1984, the same year that DH Homes was dissolved."

"That makes sense," Eric said, nodding.

Carly pulled another document out of her file. "Not only did I find the deed from when Emil Humphrey purchased a property on Sunset Lane in Rhinelander, Wisconsin, but I found out that the family still owns that property."

"Emil is still alive?"

"I don't think so," Carly said, shaking her head. "The property is held in a trust now, and Emil's two sons, Phillip and Donald, are listed as the trustees."

"Are you going to talk to them too?"

"I'm not ruling it out, but I'm not sure what I would gain by talking to them."

"You really found out a lot of stuff," Eric said.

"Oh, that's not all." Carly's eyes sparkled with excitement. She looked like she had just won the biggest race of the year. "I found a birth certificate for Timothy Eugene Holt," she said. "He was born on January 21, 1926, in Saguenay, Quebec, Canada. I got a death certificate from the Canadian Army indicating that he died on April 4, 1945, in the Netherlands. You were right about the date. He's buried in the Beny-sur-Mer Canadian Cemetery in Normandy."

Eric nodded slowly, taking it all in.

"I also found a birth certificate for his sister, Florence," she said. "She was eighteen years older than him. Because he died so young, there wasn't much else to find out about him. There was no marriage license or any kind of property records."

Eric stared up at the ceiling, the textured surface blurring slightly as he processed the information. Then a new memory surfaced. "I was left-handed when I was Tim." He chuckled softly. "I just remembered."

Carly laughed along with him, then pressed forward. "Unfortunately, I haven't had much luck getting any documentation from when you were Cornelius Hopper in England," she said. "I've requested the records but haven't received anything yet."

"What about my life in Colorado?" Eric noticed that it was now much easier for him to refer to his memories as 'my life as…' Had he accepted that what he was remembering was actually his own past lives? He didn't think so, but the more he spoke to Carly, the easier it was to entertain the possibility.

Carly hesitated. "I found out a couple of things, but I have more questions for you about that life."

"Sure, what do you need to know?" he asked.

"Tell me more about your wife and your marriage."

Eric's lips curved into a soft smile, his thoughts bringing back pleasant memories of a life he hadn't known existed just a few months earlier. "Out of everything I remember from that life, my memories of my marriage are the strongest. My wife's name was Rachel Barrett. Her father was the ranch owner I worked for, E.J. Barrett. I asked him if I could marry Rachel before I asked her. He had taken me under his wing, and although I was just a ranch hand, he treated me like a partner. When Rachel and I were married, E.J. and I built a small home for us right on the ranch."

"Tell me more about Rachel."

Eric smiled "In my memory, Rachel was beautiful, with strawberry blond hair, freckles across her cheeks, and the cutest gap-toothed smile." His gaze softened as he spoke. "She used to wear different colored ribbons in her hair. She'd wear a different color every day. I used to tell her that her ribbons and her smile could brighten up even the darkest day. She had a great sense of humor, and she liked to tease me. She was slim, but she was a hard worker. She could keep up with the hands when it came to working cattle. Like her father, she was kind and friendly, but she could be tough as nails. And she had a stubborn streak." He paused a moment, remembering the woman he had once loved. "I feel an affection for Rachel unlike anyone else I remember from any of my other lives."

"I can tell from the way you talk about her," Carly said, her voice soft and filled with emotion.

"We weren't married very long before she died. Maybe two years. But my love for her went on until the day I died. I never remarried. I didn't have any interest in seeing any other women. I knew no one else could ever replace her."

Carly stared at Eric until it became uncomfortable for him.

"Is something wrong?" he asked.

She began to speak but had to clear her throat and start again. "No, it's just that…it's very romantic," she said. "I want to look into your Colorado life more. When I get the information, I'll let you know. For now, the documentation I've gathered is very promising." She gathered up her tablet and her files, then stood.

Eric followed her lead and also stood. "Promising?" he asked. "I'm not sure what you mean."

"I'm sorry. It's probably selfish of me to think of it that way," she said. "What I've been able to find so far is very good information that is going to make a fabulous report. I'm going to submit my findings to an academic journal, and I'll likely speak about my findings at industry conferences. What you've told me and what I've been able to document is really going to add to the literature on past life research."

"That's great," he said, although his voice carried a hint of concern. "Just great."

CHAPTER 21

Eric and Michelle ordered dinner, and the server brought Michelle a second glass of wine. The warm, golden glow from the overhead lights reflected off the wine's surface, casting flickering shadows onto the white tablecloth. She took a long drink, savoring the crisp taste, then set her glass down, spinning the glass and amusedly watching the patterns that were being cast on the table.

"Why aren't you drinking tonight?" she asked, tilting her head curiously.

"It's counterproductive to my training."

"But it's the offseason," she said. "Aren't you supposed to ease up?"

"You know I can't ease up. I go in for my IndyCar Medical evaluation next week."

Michelle nodded, a small frown creasing her forehead as she took another sip of her wine. Eric could see the wheels turning in her mind, but he chose not to press her.

Out of the corner of his eye, Eric spotted his fellow driver, Conor Daly, at a table across the room. Conor waved, his broad grin unmistakable even from a distance. Eric returned the greeting with a nod and a quick lift of his hand.

Michelle turned in her seat to follow his gaze, then turned back toward Eric. "Is that Conor?"

Eric nodded. "It is."

"Who's that woman he's with?"

"His girlfriend, I think."

"Are you sure?" Michelle asked, her eyebrows arching slightly. "I thought his girlfriend was a redhead."

Eric shrugged, his attention drifting back to Michelle. "Listen, there's something I want to talk to you about." He sat up straighter, his voice filled with enthusiasm and the prospect of sharing some news with Michelle. He also felt a little *I told you so* energy, though he didn't want to admit it to himself.

"Whatever it is, you seem excited about it." A hint of a smile played on her lips, but her eyes remained cautious.

"A little bit," Eric admitted, trying to tamp down what he was feeling. He took a deep breath and leaned forward slightly. "Dr. Pellegrino did her investigation and found that most of what I've been remembering is real."

Michelle's expression remained neutral, but her eyes darkened noticeably. "What does that mean?"

"It means that she was able to document the things that I told her," he said. "The people I'm remembering were real. The places I was born and where I lived were real."

"Her research doesn't mean a thing." She used air quotes when she said the word "research." "What's the difference if the people and places are real? If I say that in a previous life, I was the Queen of England and you look it up, and sure enough, there's such a place as England and they have a Queen, that doesn't mean I must be telling the truth. Everything Pellegrino found is public record. It's on the internet. Maybe you came across the information while surfing the internet and you're just remembering what you read." She leaned her elbows on the table and stared into Eric's eyes. "Plus, you told me you weren't going to be seeing Pellegrino anymore."

"I never said I wasn't going to see her," he said, his tone defensive. "I said I was done interviewing with her."

"Whatever," Michelle said, waving her hand dismissively. "It's still ridiculous to think that she is anything but a fraud."

Eric felt the urge to defend Carly, but he knew there was nothing he could say to convince Michelle. Plus, Carly wasn't the issue. His memories and the documentation she found were the issue. It irritated him that Michelle was dismissing out of hand what he was telling her.

His voice rose slightly. "How are Dr. Pellegrino's findings any more ridiculous than your theory that I read something on the internet and now I'm remembering those things as if they're my own memories?"

Michelle glanced around the restaurant, her eyes darting toward the nearby tables. She leaned in, lowering her voice. "You need to give up these reincarnation fantasies," she said. "People around the sport are starting to talk. I didn't want to say anything about it, but I've heard whispers around the paddock. You don't have a ride for next year, Eric. If word gets out about your strange memories and your belief that you're remembering past lives, you'll never get another contract. What team is going to sign a driver recovering from head trauma that has memories of other people's lives living in his head and claims he's been reincarnated?"

Eric took Michelle's cue and lowered his voice, but the heat of the moment remained. "How would people within the sport know anything about my memories or what I believe?"

Michelle sat back in her chair, her eyes widening. "What? You think I told them?"

Eric was surprised Michelle assumed he was pointing the finger at her. That hadn't been his intention. "No, that's not what I'm saying."

Her tone softened. "I would hope you know me better than that," she said. "It's more likely that Pellegrino told Dr. Ferris and Dr. Ferris told IndyCar Medical. They're probably the ones that leaked the information to the paddock." Michelle's tone shifted again, this time to something almost maternal. "I'm just looking out for you, babe. You need a job for next year, and no one is going to sign a driver who thinks he remembers his past lives."

"Why wouldn't they?" he asked, frustration creeping back into his voice. "There are plenty of other drivers who believe in UFOs or ghosts or Bigfoot, yet they have jobs. Hell, I think Will Power believes in all that stuff."

"But they didn't develop those beliefs after suffering a traumatic brain injury from a racing accident captured live on national TV. No team is going to take a risk that your injury is going to lead to even weirder behavior. What sponsor is going to pay to have their brand associated with you and your memories?"

Eric leaned back in his chair and shook his head. Her words stung, not because they were cruel, but because they might be true. He wanted to protest, to push back against the picture Michelle was painting, but a part of him feared she was right.

"Eric, you know how the game is played." Michelle's tone was resolute. "Name one person in the series that is there solely because they're a great driver. You have to be media savvy and corporate friendly, as well as a world class driver. If you can't represent the sponsor without embarrassing them, they'll find someone else to support. It's their money. They get to make the rules. You need to drop this past life nonsense. For the sake of your career. And for us."

CHAPTER 22

Eric grabbed a towel and wiped sweat from his face. The fabric felt rough against his flushed skin, soaking up the sweat from a demanding workout. "It feels great to be training again," he said to Justin, his trainer. His breath came in short bursts. "It feels good to be pushing myself again."

"You've been doing great." Justin clapped Eric on the back, the gesture meant as much to jostle as to encourage. "I think you'll pass that IndyCar physical with flying colors."

Eric picked up his workout bag and slung it over his shoulder as he headed for the door. "I hope you're right. Just a few more days."

Getting back into a workout routine had been far from easy. His muscles had atrophied, leaving him a shadow of his former self. His stamina, once a point of pride, had dwindled alarmingly. The muscles in his neck—those crucial pillars of strength for a race car driver—had grown weak and stiff. But weeks of focused work with Justin were paying off. His body, though still a work in progress, was showing signs of resilience. Each session left him feeling a little stronger, a little closer to the driver he used to be.

Sliding into the driver's seat of his car, Eric tossed his workout bag onto the passenger seat. He fished his phone out of the bag, its screen lighting up to reveal a missed call from Carly. Again. That made three calls in the past two days. He hadn't been answering or returning her calls, even though he wanted to. He couldn't shake the echoes of Michelle's warnings. What if his association with Carly and her past life research jeopardized his chances of getting a new contract?

His finger hovered over the screen as he considered calling Carly back. But just as he was about to set the phone down, it buzzed in his hand. "Johan" flashed on the screen. His manager.

"I have some news for you," Johan said, his voice brisk and businesslike.

Eric straightened in his seat, gripping the phone a little tighter. "I hope it's good news."

"It might be," Johan said. "I was talking to Robert Perry last night. Team Perry has an open seat for next year, and Robert would like to talk to you about it."

Eric's heart skipped a beat. "Robert Perry?" He hardly dared to believe what he was hearing. Team Perry was one of the top teams in the sport. "I thought that seat was taken by Hugo Renz."

"Turns out Hugo has some legal issues hanging over his head in Brazil," Johan explained. "You know how strait-laced Perry is. Once he found out, he cut off negotiations. The seat's still open, and it's a great opportunity. What do you think?"

"What do I think?" Eric's voice brimmed with barely restrained excitement. "I think I want that seat."

"That's what I thought you'd say." Johan let out a chuckle. "Robert said he wants to set something up soon. I'll call him back and let you know when and where we'll meet."

When the call ended, Eric leaned back against the seat, a rush of adrenaline coursing through him. "Team Perry," he murmured to himself, the name carrying a weight of possibility and promise. His pulse quickened at the thought. Team Perry was the kind of team race car drivers dreamed of; a powerhouse with the cars, the personnel, and the resources to win races and be perennial championship contenders. Securing a seat with them would be a game-changer.

For a fleeting moment, he considered returning Carly's calls but now pushed the thought aside. He couldn't afford any distractions, any potential controversies that might complicate his path to Team Perry.

Michelle's voice echoed in his mind, her warnings about appearances and reputations taking on a new gravity. For now, Carly would have to wait.

CHAPTER 23

The restaurant was upscale, with dark wood paneling and soft lighting that created an intimate atmosphere. Robert had reserved a back room at the restaurant, allowing for a private conversation and servers that focused exclusively on him and his guests. Robert, Johan, and Eric shared a table in the middle of the room. Twice as many servers stood by to wait on them.

Eric's steak was perfectly cooked, and the wine Robert chose complemented the meal beautifully. The easy flow of conversation gave Eric the confidence that this meeting might end with a handshake and the promise of a new contract. Now, with the meeting winding down, Eric was starting to think that the seat at Team Perry was his.

"We haven't really spoken much about your accident at Indy last year." Robert leaned back in his chair and folded his hands in his lap. His tone was casual, but his sharp eyes betrayed his genuine interest. "What can you tell me about it?"

Eric's chest tightened. He'd hoped the topic wouldn't come up. He kept his tone measured. "There's not much to say that you probably don't already know," he said. "A suspension component on the left front failed, and it sent me into the wall. I suffered a fractured skull and a broken neck. Thankfully, my recovery has been quick and complete. No lingering effects at all."

"Are you sure about no lingering effects?" Robert's voice was calm but there was an edge to it. "I've heard that after the accident, you started having strange memories about things that never happened to you, and that doctors can't explain those memories."

Eric swallowed hard, his throat dry. He glanced across the table at Johan, who squirmed in his chair, suddenly unable to get comfortable. Eric's heart raced. "I did have some odd memories that I couldn't explain right after the accident, but they've subsided since then. It's not an issue at this point." He forced himself to hold Robert's gaze and smile, but he feared that his expression betrayed his unease.

Robert's lips curled into a thin smile. "The reason I ask is that I was talking to your friend Michelle the other day, and she mentioned that you had been seeing some psychic who had convinced you that you were experiencing memories from past lives."

"Michelle told you that?" Eric asked, his voice barely above a whisper. A mix of disbelief and anger churned in his stomach, but his outward demeanor remained calm and friendly.

Robert crossed one leg over the other. "I was talking to her about doing some PR work for the team when she mentioned it."

Johan leaned forward in his seat. "Michelle must be mistaken."

Without looking at him, Robert raised a hand, a subtle but firm gesture to silence Johan. "I appreciate that, but I'd like to hear what Eric has to say."

Eric's jaw tightened as he fought to maintain his composure. How could Michelle have betrayed him like this? He pushed the thought aside, focusing on damage control. "After the accident, I was treated by Dr. Ferris at Indiana Methodist." Eric's voice was carefully measured. "He asked me to follow up with Dr. Pellegrino. She's a psychologist, not a psychic. We talked a couple of times, but nothing came of it. I haven't spoken to her since. I think Michelle might be confused about what actually happened."

Robert's expression softened slightly, though his eyes remained analytical. "That's good," he said. "You know, anything weird like that can drive sponsors away. Can you imagine a sponsor wanting to associate themselves with that kind of mumbo jumbo?"

Eric forced a laugh, the sound hollow in his own ears. "Of course."

Robert slid his chair back and stood, extending a hand to Eric. "I enjoyed our evening, gentlemen. I'll be in touch." He shook hands with both Eric and Johan, his grip firm but quick, and was gone before Eric had fully processed the interaction.

As Robert disappeared into the dimly lit hallway leading out of the restaurant, Johan turned to Eric, his expression a mixture of frustration and concern. "What the hell is Michelle doing telling Robert something like that about you?"

Eric's eyes burned with hurt and anger. "I don't know," he said, his voice low and tense. "But I intend to find out."

CHAPTER 24

It was a warm night in Indianapolis despite being early November. Eric sat in his car with the air conditioning running, his mind reeling. His gaze fixed on Michelle's apartment building, the lights in the windows glowing faintly against the darkness. The anger simmered in his chest. He thought about going home, taking the time to sleep on it, but he knew he wouldn't feel any different after a good night's sleep. The anger would fester, and sleep would elude him. What Michelle had done could not be overlooked.

He took a deep breath and turned the ignition off, the sudden silence giving the night an ominous feeling. He stepped out of the car, the warm night air enveloped him.

Each step to the front door felt deliberate, weighed down, as if his body resisted the confrontation he knew was coming. He rang the bell, his heart pounding against his ribs. Michelle opened the door, her hair pinned up. She wore a loose-fitting T-shirt with Pato O'Ward's picture on the front, and a pair of orange shorts. Even when she was dressed down like this, which wasn't often, she still exuded confidence and poise.

"Eric," she said, her brow furrowing slightly. "I was just getting ready for bed. Is everything okay?"

"Can I come in?" he asked, his voice steady but clipped. It wasn't lost on him that he still had to ask to be let in, while Michelle walked freely into his home whenever she pleased.

"Sure." She stepped aside and held the door open.

Eric walked past her, entering the pristine apartment. As always, the place was immaculate. The furniture was perfectly arranged, the surfaces spotless, the air faintly scented with lavender. It felt more like a showroom than a person's home, sterile and curated, as if Michelle lived her life always prepared for someone else's scrutiny.

"How did your meeting go with Robert?" She closed the door behind him.

Eric turned to face her. "It went okay, but…" He hesitated, taking a deep breath. "Michelle, you told Robert about my memories."

Her eyes widened, and she gasped softly. "What do you mean? No, I didn't."

Eric sighed, running a hand through his hair, an attempt to ground himself. "Yes, you did, Michelle. Robert asked me about my memories and said that you were the one who told him about them."

"No, I…" Michelle stammered, her confidence faltering for a moment. "I'm not…" She stopped, the weight of the accusation sinking in. "It's not what you think. I was talking to Robert about possibly taking over their PR work next season. I didn't just blurt it out. I was trying to explain your situation and how I…"

"So, you did tell him?" Eric's voice cut through the tension in the room.

Michelle fell heavily into a wing chair, one that looked as though it had never been sat in before. She tilted her head back and exhaled forcefully, her facade of poise crumbling. "I didn't mean to," she said. "It just slipped out."

"Slipped out?" he repeated, his words thick with disbelief. "How does something like that just 'slip out'?"

Her eyes darted to his, defiant for a moment, as if ready to defend herself. But then her shoulders slumped, and she sighed deeply. "I don't know," she said. Her voice was barely above a whisper. "It was an accident."

Eric shook his head slowly, his movements deliberate as he began pacing the room. "You were so concerned about how the paddock would react if they knew about my memories," he said. "You wanted me to stop trying to figure out what was going on. You wanted me to stop seeing Dr. Pellegrino so my secret didn't get out. And then you go and tell one of the most well-connected people in the sport to help yourself get a job."

Tears welled up in Michelle's eyes, her composure cracking. "I'm sorry, Eric." Her voice trembled. "I didn't mean to. I'm so sorry."

Eric stopped pacing and turned to look her in the eyes. He hesitated, his anger warring with his sense of fairness. "I can't trust you."

"Yes, you can, babe" she said quickly, her desperation spilling over. "Of course you can."

He shook his head. "No, Michelle, I can't." He made a swirling gesture with his hand near his ear. "I don't know what's going on in my head, what these memories are all about, but I'm going to find out. And while I'm doing that, I can't have people I don't trust in my life."

"No, Eric. No…" Michelle's voice broke as she began to sob. "You don't mean that."

Eric nodded slowly. He stared at her for a moment, his expression pained but resolute. "I do." He walked to the door. "I have to go," he said softly. He opened the door and stepped out into the warm Indianapolis night.

Chapter 25

When Eric woke the morning after his and Michelle's breakup, the clarity of his choice settled over him like the day's first light. He knew he had done the right thing. But it still felt strange to have jettisoned Michelle from his life, as though an anchor had been cut, leaving him adrift yet lighter. Her absence was like a fresh wound from a life-saving surgery, painful but necessary

Sitting at his kitchen table with a cup of coffee in his hands, Eric felt an unexpected urge to call Carly. He owed her an apology for not returning her calls these past few days. He owed her an explanation, too, for why he couldn't participate anymore in her research. It was a conversation he dreaded but one he knew he couldn't avoid.

He picked up his phone from the table and dialed her number. When her voice came on the line, it was warm but tinged with concern.

"Eric, is everything okay?" she asked. "I was worried when you didn't return my calls."

"Everything's fine." He forced a brightness into his tone. "I've just been super busy trying to get back into shape. I'm meeting with IndyCar doctors in a few days, and I want to be ready." The excuse sounded hollow even to him, and a pang of guilt twisted in his chest. Carly didn't deserve to be lied to.

If she detected his unease or was bothered by his lazy lie, she didn't let on. "I have news to share with you." Her voice lifting with excitement. "I've been able to track down some additional information, and I'm working on a paper detailing my findings. A lot of exciting things are going on. Can we get together to talk about it all?"

Eric closed his eyes, exhaling slowly before answering. "I'm sorry, Carly. I can't really talk about this anymore with you. I hope you understand."

There was a pause on the other end of the line. When Carly spoke, her voice was quieter, tinged with confusion. "I'm not sure what you mean."

"My manager and I are talking to a couple of different teams about driving for them next year," he explained. "I need to be careful about how I present myself."

"I don't understand," she said. "What do your contract negotiations have to do with our work?"

Eric rubbed the back of his neck, searching for the right words. "Sponsors pay a lot of money to be associated with a team and its driver," he said. "The last thing they want to do is to spend millions of dollars on a sponsorship only to learn that the driver they're linked with is into some crazy conspiracy theory."

There was a beat of silence. "Conspiracy theory?" Carly asked. Her tone shifted. She didn't sound defensive or angry, just hurt. "Is that what you think of my work? Some crazy conspiracy theory?"

Eric's stomach tightened. "No, that's not what I think," he said. He felt the weight of his words, the unintended blow they'd dealt. "You're doing important work, work that most people don't understand. I certainly don't understand it. It's all new to me. And even though I'm interested in your work, sponsors don't want to associate their brand with my memories or allusions to reincarnation. There are plenty of teams and drivers looking for sponsorship money. The sponsors don't want to risk the money on someone with the kind of baggage I have."

"It's not baggage, Eric. It's a gift." Carly's voice was earnest but insistent. "Most people are closed off from their past life memories. But for you, the walls have come down, and you've been allowed to see the person you were in previous lives."

Eric let out a long sigh, running a hand through his hair. He appreciated Carly's passion, her conviction, but she didn't understand what this was costing him. "It's not a gift, Carly. At least for me, it's a curse," he said. "I don't want to remember these things. I want my old life back, where I didn't have to deal with all of this."

There was a pause before Carly responded. "I can't pretend to understand how this must be impacting you," she said. "And I certainly don't understand how it affects your driving career. But I promise you, Eric, it is a gift. You may not see that now, but it truly is a gift."

Eric's shoulders sagged. He hated disappointing Carly, hated the way her belief in him only seemed to amplify his own doubts. "If it's a gift, it's one I can't accept," he said. "At least not now. I'm really sorry, Carly, but I can't talk to you about this anymore. Good luck with your paper. But please, don't use my name."

The silence that followed was heavy, weighted with unspoken words. Eric could feel the hurt he had inflicted. It made his heart ache for her, but he knew he couldn't repair the damage he had caused, not while he was still looking for a new contract.

He closed his eyes. "I'll talk to you later."

CHAPTER 26

When Eric woke, it was still dark. He tossed and turned for an hour or more, then finally decided to climb out of bed. The stillness of the house amplified his thoughts, turning each into a dagger that was sharp and threatening. He shuffled through the darkened living room, his bare feet brushing against the cool wood floor. Sitting heavily on the couch, he grabbed the television remote. But instead of turning the TV on, he let the remote fall back onto the coffee table with a soft clatter, then leaned into the couch cushions, staring into the dim shadows of the room.

He took a deep breath and closed his eyes. He didn't have a job, no longer had a girlfriend, and his uninvited memories were threatening to take over his life. The fear that this chaotic new reality might be his permanent normal gnawed at him like a wild animal. And so far, he couldn't figure out how to keep the animal at bay.

Pulling his legs up onto the couch, he laid his head against a throw pillow, the fabric rough against his cheek. His body craved more sleep, but his mind refused to rest. He exhaled and commanded his body to relax, though the tension lingered.

Suddenly, he was in deep, rough water, the waves battering him as he struggled to keep his head above the surface. A weight pressed heavily on his back, dragging him down. He was next to a landing craft, and men poured out of it into the water, their shouts and the sound of gunfire cutting through the chaos. The impact of bodies colliding with his sent him tumbling below the surface, saltwater burning his throat. He clawed at the straps of his pack and rifle, desperate to shed the weight, but his waterlogged body refused to cooperate. The surf churned above him, relentless, and he felt his lungs burning, his strength fading.

In the darkness, he thought of Florence. He wanted to go home. He wanted to see her one last time.

A sharp sound pierced the scene, and Eric opened his eyes, gasping for breath. The phone on the coffee table buzzed again, the vibration rattling against the wood. He blinked, his heart still pounding from the vivid vision. Snagging the phone, he cleared his throat and answered.

"Did I wake you?" Johan asked.

"No, I got out of bed an hour ago." Although it wasn't exactly a lie, he didn't want to go into the mechanics of the whole truth.

"I have some news for you."

Eric sat up, shaking his head to clear the lingering cobwebs. "What is it?"

"I have good and not-so-good news. Which do you want first?"

Eric wasn't interested in turning this into a game, but he played along just the same. "The good news."

"The good news is that IndyCar Medical signed off on your physical," Johan said. "You're eligible to race again."

Eric wasn't surprised. He had gone through the physical process two days earlier and hadn't sensed any concerns from the doctors. Even so, it was good to hear the official approval. "That is good news," he said. "At least my physical health won't be a question mark when we talk to teams about next year. What's the not-so-good news?"

"I heard back from Robert Perry," Johan said. "Team Perry has decided to go with another driver for their open seat."

"Who did they go with?"

"Robert didn't say, although I expect the team will make an announcement in the next day or two."

Eric sighed, the disappointment washing over him and adding to the unraveling that was taking place in his life. "After the way our meeting with Robert ended, that isn't a huge surprise."

"No, but I still held out hope."

"What do we do now?"

"I have some calls to make," Johan said. "There are still a few good seats available. I'll get busy and keep you posted."

When they hung up, Eric slumped back on the couch, letting out a loud groan. The image of drowning when he was Tim Holt gave way to the present-day disappointment of losing out on the job with Team Perry. Like Johan, despite how the dinner had ended, he had held onto a sliver of hope that things might still work out. He allowed himself a brief pity party, then pushed himself up off the couch. "I need coffee," he muttered to the empty room.

At the coffee shop, the drive-thru was backed up, so Eric decided to go inside. The rich aroma of freshly brewed coffee greeted him as he joined the line. It seemed everyone in town needed their caffeine fix at the exact same time.

"Hi, Eric."

The familiar voice made him turn, and there she was. Michelle stood a few feet away, her posture slightly hesitant. Her smile was polite but guarded.

"Oh, hi," he said.

"How have you been?"

She had called and texted a few times in the two weeks since they'd split, but he hadn't responded. Now, standing before her, he felt an odd detachment. The usual pull he had felt toward her was gone, replaced by a quiet indifference.

"I'm good. How about you?" he asked.

"I'm okay." Her voice lacked the confidence he was used to. She twirled a strand of hair around her finger, her eyes darting away from his. "Did you hear back from Team Perry yet?"

"Yeah." He shook his head. "I didn't get the seat."

Although it went unmentioned, the tension between them was thick with the understanding that her actions had played a role in the outcome. It was a betrayal he couldn't forgive.

"I'm really sorry, Eric," she said, her voice soft.

He nodded curtly. "Uh huh." He bit his lip. "How about you? Did they give you their PR work?"

She shook her head. "No, I didn't get the job. I'm still looking."

Eric opened his mouth to offer a hollow "I'm sorry," but before he could speak, a man a couple of inches taller than him approached, handing Michelle a cup of coffee.

"Ready to go?" the man asked.

Michelle smiled at him and nodded. She turned back to Eric. "It was nice seeing you."

"You too."

Michelle and the man left the coffee shop, and Eric turned back toward the counter. The barista was waiting to take his order.

"That was awkward," Eric said, managing a wry smile.

The barista grinned. "I've seen worse."

Chapter 27

When Johan told him that they were going to meet with Kevin Butler from Hardy-Butler Racing, Eric wasn't particularly excited. Hardy-Butler had only been in the series for four or five years, and they had never won a race or been particularly competitive.

Hardy-Butler had a reputation as a team that gave new drivers their initial break in IndyCar. They were a team where drivers went to learn, not to win. When he protested, Johan laughed.

"I thought you might say that," Johan said. "Let's just hear him out and see what he has to offer."

Now, having spent the evening talking to Kevin Butler, Eric felt differently about the prospect of driving for him. The team was clearly growing, and they were much better funded than they had been in their early years. Kevin himself was much more down-to-earth and personable than Robert Perry had been. Even more so than Clint.

"I can offer as much money as any other team," Kevin said. "I can provide you with a competitive car, a state-of-the-art race shop, and a top-notch crew. What I can't give you is a résumé of victories or championships. We haven't achieved those goals yet. But trust me, we have those goals, and we're getting close. With you in the fold, I think we can achieve them."

Eric nodded, impressed by Kevin's candor. He had expected lofty promises, the kind that usually accompanied such pitches, but Kevin's honesty felt refreshing. "I like what I'm hearing," Eric said.

"I'll submit a formal offer to Johan tomorrow. If everything looks good to the two of you, we'll have a deal."

"Sounds great," Eric said, a cautious optimism taking root.

"One final thing." Kevin leaned back in his chair. "I'd like to cap this evening off with a final drink." He waved the waiter over to their table.

They each ordered another drink, the atmosphere in the room positive and upbeat. Eric caught himself relaxing, his earlier reservations about Hardy-Butler dissipating with each passing moment.

"I've been wanting to ask you about something," Kevin said after the waiter left to fetch their drink order. "But I wanted to get the business stuff out of the way first."

Eric's stomach tightened. The night had gone so well, and he had hoped he'd dodged the inevitable question about his past life memories. Now, he feared it would ruin the great rapport he'd built with Kevin. "Sure, what's that?" he asked, keeping his tone neutral but fearing the worst.

"I heard you've been looking into reincarnation and your past lives." Kevin's voice was curious rather than accusatory.

Eric saw no reason to downplay it. The story was out there, and everyone in the paddock had heard about it by now. "I have," Eric said, meeting Kevin's gaze directly. "Is that a problem?"

"Why would it be a problem?" Kevin's face broke into a grin. "I'm a believer. Have been for years. My wife is a Buddhist, and she introduced me to the concept when we first started dating. It just makes sense to me."

"No kidding?" Eric's eyebrows shot up in surprise. "That's good to hear."

Before Kevin could elaborate further, the waiter returned with their drinks. Kevin raised his glass and offered a toast.

"To a successful partnership," Kevin said.

Eric clinked his glass against Kevin's. "I'll drink to that."

Chapter 28

Eric reluctantly agreed to sit for an interview with Brady Collins from the *Indianapolis Star*. He didn't particularly like doing interviews, but his signing with Hardy-Butler Racing was news, and it was good PR for the team and their new sponsor, FeeGo Streaming Services, an internet streaming service.

Brady Collins was well-known in IndyCar circles for being tough but fair in his questioning, always well-prepared, and, although he worked for a local newspaper, his columns and features were widely read throughout the country. He had a reputation for getting drivers to open up, often coaxing out stories that no one else could.

Brady had reserved the back room of a coffee shop in downtown Indianapolis. The room was small but tastefully decorated with dark wood wainscotting on the walls, accented by colorful original prints from local artists. The warm lighting and subtle buzz of activity in the main café created a cozy atmosphere that felt worlds away from the high-octane chaos of the racetrack.

"Some fans were surprised to hear that you signed with Hardy-Butler." Brady leaned forward in his chair, his note pad open in front of him. "You're kind of a big-name driver, and Hardy-Butler—no offense meant—is kind of a small-name team. How did it come about?"

Eric smiled faintly, his hands clasped loosely on the table. "I might agree with you if I had signed a couple of years ago. Hardy-Butler was still a new team then, and they were just finding their footing in the series. Truthfully, I'm not sure I would have been interested in driving for them at the time. But the team has grown in experience and personnel, and in the last year or two, we've seen them become increasingly competitive. I think they're on the verge of taking that next big step where they're consistently competing for podiums and race wins, and I feel really fortunate to be the guy who's going to be behind the wheel for it all."

Brady nodded thoughtfully. The small recorder on the table captured every word, but he also took notes on a yellow legal pad, his pen moving quickly across the paper. When he finished scribbling, he looked back at Eric.

"Let's turn that question around a little bit," Brady said, crossing one leg over the other. "Despite your success, you haven't raced since Indianapolis last year. You've been dealing with some significant injuries, and you were only recently cleared by IndyCar Medical to return to racing action. Do you view Hardy-Butler as taking a risk putting you in their car?"

Eric cringed. The old adage rang in his head: *You're only as good as your last race.* And his last race had ended with him being airlifted to a hospital.

Eric straightened in his chair. "If it's a risk, I don't think it's much of one. I have a six-year record of success in this series, and I don't think one accident is going to change that, especially considering that it was a mechanical failure, not driver error, that led to the accident at Indy."

Brady took more notes. He leaned forward slightly, resting his elbows on the table. "Your physical injuries from the accident appear to be healed. IndyCar Medical says you're physically able to resume racing activities. But what about the mental or emotional injuries? I've been hearing stories that you've been experiencing unexplained memories ever since the accident and that you've been seeing a psychic who believes the memories are proof of reincarnation."

There it was. The secret that had spread through the paddock had now made its way to the general public. Eric wanted to get up and leave, but that would look terrible and would only give the story more traction. Instead, he decided to play it off as best he could.

He forced a laugh. "I'm afraid you have the story a little confused." He kept his voice casual, making it sound like he found the rumors humorous. "I'm not seeing a psychic. She's a psychologist. Her name is Dr. Carly Pellegrino. She's a researcher."

Eric took a breath, choosing his words carefully.

"These memories, or whatever they are, aren't unpleasant or disruptive. They're kind of like your memory of what you had for dinner last night or what you did last weekend. You remember those things, but they don't control your life. I can't explain them, but they're nothing to be concerned about."

"What about this idea that you're remembering past lives?"

Eric sighed and shrugged, his shoulders relaxing slightly. "I don't know what to tell you about that," he said. "I don't really know much about reincarnation, and I don't think there's any way to say one way or the other if, one, reincarnation is real, and two, if what I'm experiencing is proof of reincarnation. I wish I could tell you more, but the truth is, reincarnation is as much a mystery to me as it is to most people."

Eric felt like he had managed to skirt the question without giving away too much.

Brady flipped to a new page in his notebook. "This year, you're going to have Greg Cairns on your pit box calling your strategy," he said. "Greg has had some success in sports cars calling races for…"

Even though Brady had moved on, Eric suddenly wanted to know more. He wasn't ready to say that he was remembering past lives, but if reincarnation was a possible explanation, he wanted to understand it better.

CHAPTER 29

Eric sat at the bar at Root & Bone, a restaurant in the Broad Ripple neighborhood of Indianapolis, admiring the overhead lights made from cut glass decanters and the tap handles made from elk antlers. He was lost in thought when Carly walked in. He almost didn't recognize her. Rather than wearing the professional clothes he had seen her wear at her office, she was dressed casually in jeans and a blue top. She wore her hair down, her dark curls falling attractively to her shoulders.

He greeted her with a smile. "You look great," he said, then realized it probably wasn't an appropriate thing to say to his psychologist. Theirs was a professional relationship, although Eric had to admit, she was on his mind more and more often, and not in a professional way.

"Thanks," she said, not seeming to mind. "I hope I didn't dress down too much."

"No. You look…I think it's fine."

They got a table and ordered fresh drinks.

"What are all these questions you have for me?" she asked.

Eric told her about the interview with the *Indianapolis Star* and how it made him realize he really didn't know anything about reincarnation. "I also don't know much about the work you do or how you got started in this field."

Carly scooted her chair closer and rested her arms on the table, tenting her hands in front of her. "Let's start with the Center for Past Life Studies," she said. "It was started by Dr. Richard Rasmussen almost thirty years ago after his young daughter began talking about how she was a policeman or a prison guard in Germany during World War II. The memories were vague, but they were not the type of memories a young girl living in 1990s America should have. There was nothing about his daughter's memories that could be investigated or confirmed, but it was enough for Dr. Rassmussen to start the Center and turn his research fully toward studying reincarnation."

"How did you get involved with the Center?"

"I've always been interested in paranormal research within the field of psychology. My dissertation at the University of Virginia was based on research I'd conducted with Dr. Brian Stevens, one of my professors. Dr. Stevens was friends with Dr. Rasmussen and was someone Dr. Rasmussen turned to for support when he started the Center. When Dr. Rasmussen needed some help, Dr. Stevens recommended that I come to work for him. I did, and when Dr. Rasmussen retired two years ago, he asked me to take over the Center."

"I have to admit, I didn't even know reincarnation was something you could study in college," Eric said. "I don't mean any offense, but it seems more like a fringe subject than something that universities would take seriously."

"Actually, you're not far off. It wasn't that long ago that reincarnation was rejected by the scientific community because there was no empirical evidence to support it as a legitimate science. Doctors Stevens and Rasmussen were pioneers. It was their work that helped to legitimize the field. I want my work to move it forward even further."

Eric took a sip of his beer, then set it on the table in front of him. Condensation covered the outside of the glass, and he wiped it with a napkin. "When the reporter for the *Star* asked me about reincarnation, I didn't know what to tell him. Can you tell me the basics?"

Carly considered Eric's question. "You probably know that reincarnation is not widely accepted in the United States. Certainly not as accepted as it is in much of the rest of the world. One of the main reasons for that is that, despite references to reincarnation in the Bible, Christians don't accept it as part of their theology."

The waiter brought fresh drinks. They each ordered dinner and wine, then the waiter left the table.

"Why is it that Christians don't accept reincarnation?" he asked.

"The main tenet of the Christian faith is that Jesus died for our sins, and it is only through belief in him and his resurrection that we can have eternal life in Heaven," she said. "By contrast, reincarnation involves a belief that we live many lives, and the purpose of being reborn over and over again is to perfect the soul." She took a sip of her wine, then continued.

"For instance, Buddhists believe that living many lives with the goal of perfecting the soul and reaching nirvana is the only way we can stop the endless cycle of birth, death, rebirth, and so on. Most other religions believe something similar."

"Christianity is the only outlier?"

"Not the only one, but one of the few. Orthodox Islam and Judaism don't teach reincarnation, but the more mystical sects of each religion do. For instance, Hasidic and Kabbalistic Judaism both have a belief in reincarnation. And the Sufi and Druze sects of Islam do as well."

Eric was intrigued. He couldn't claim to know much about the various religions, but he had attended church back in Florida when he was a kid and had always considered himself a Christian, even if it didn't play a particularly large role in his life. "Does Christianity have any sects that believe in reincarnation?"

Carly thought for a moment. "This is kind of confusing, so bear with me," she said. "Early Christians believed in reincarnation. They were influenced by Christian thinkers such as Origen of Alexandria, who, in turn influenced later thinkers like St. Clement and Justin Martyr. But in a meeting of church leaders designed to unite the various Christian sects, they condemned Origen and removed reincarnation from the canon of Christian beliefs. Even so, some modern Christian thinkers point to various verses in the Bible and interpret them to refer to reincarnation."

"I've never heard most of what you just said, including those names you mentioned."

Carly nodded. "Most of what I just told you is not well-known to the vast majority of Christians. But because of Christianity's history with renouncing reincarnation, in the United States, it's viewed as taboo. We don't talk about it much, and when we do, it's often viewed as a bonkers theory only believed by hippies and new age charlatans. But outside the Western world, reincarnation is accepted as a fact of what happens after we die."

Eric took a sip of his drink. "What does happen when we die?"

Carly laughed. "That's a big question."

The waiter brought their meals and a fresh glass of wine for each of them. Eric offered a toast. "To your research."

Carly clinked glasses with Eric. "You're pretty involved in that research at the moment."

"To our research," he said.

Carly laughed again. "I wouldn't go that far."

"So, come on, professor. What happens when we die?"

Carly took a bite of her salmon and chewed thoughtfully. "The short answer is, we don't know. At least, not for certain. But what believers in reincarnation think happens is that we go into a kind of holding pattern where we review the life we've just lived and prepare to be reborn into an existence that suits our soul. While we're in this holding pattern, we look to be reborn into a life that will provide the kind of experiences we need to grow and develop."

"So, we choose what body and situation we're going to be born into?" he asked.

"It's hard to say," Carly said. "But there is research that tends to support the idea that the soul does not enter the body until the moment of birth. It's thought that one of the reasons for this is for the soul to better understand the body and life they are joining. It allows the soul to make an informed decision about its next journey, though it's not always as deliberate as it sounds."

Eric set his fork down, his expression shifting from curiosity to something deeper, more pensive. "So, we have some sort of say in how our next life unfolds?"

"Maybe," Carly said, tilting her head thoughtfully. "But it's not like selecting items off a menu. The choice seems to be more about aligning with the circumstances that will provide the challenges or lessons the soul needs for growth. It's less about want and more about necessity."

"Necessity," Eric repeated softly. His mind churned, caught between the weight of the concept and the strange resonance it brought to his own fragmented memories. "That's... intense."

Carly smiled faintly. "It is. But it's also liberating if you think about it. The hardships we face in life may not be random. They could be opportunities, even if they don't feel that way in the moment."

Eric let out a small laugh, though it lacked humor. "That's a nice way to frame it. But it's hard to swallow when you're in the thick of it."

"Of course," Carly said. "No one's saying it's easy. It's just... a different way to view the struggles we all face."

"This idea that we choose the life and the body we want to be in, and we don't do it until the moment of birth is new to me," he said. "I've never run across that way of thinking before."

"A lot of Americans don't like the idea that the soul doesn't enter the body until birth. We've been programmed to believe over the years that the soul is attached to the body from the moment of conception. There's no evidence to back up that theory, but there is evidence to support the idea that the soul enters the body later in the process, maybe as late as at the moment of birth."

"What evidence are you talking about?" he asked.

"There's only a small amount of evidence, and what there is, is anecdotal," she said. "In doing interviews while I was at the University of Virginia, I spoke to kids in India that remembered visiting their parents before birth to see if they were a good fit. The kids remembered staying detached from the body until the moment of birth. Research done by others in the field has produced similar results."

Eric nodded thoughtfully, considering Carly's words. "Anything else you can tell me?"

Carly thought for a moment. "There are a couple of things. For instance, there's a school of thought that suggests we live more than one life at a time, just on different timelines. That's a little outside my area of research, but I find the possibility fascinating."

"That's crazy," Eric said. "I mean, in a good way." He took a bite of his shrimp and grits. "Why don't we remember past lives. Or, I guess, why am I suddenly remembering mine?"

"Memory is stored in the hippocampus of the brain," she said. "It's believed that as the brain develops, we build up a wall in the hippocampus to block out memories of past lives. That's why we usually see past life memories come from young children—usually from about three-to-eight-years-old—because their brains haven't developed sufficiently to build those walls. I'm guessing the brain trauma you suffered in the accident somehow broke down or disrupted that wall. If I had to guess, I'd say the wall is probably being rebuilt, and in a year or two, maybe three, those past life memories will be gone."

"You think these memories will eventually go away?"

"I'm guessing they will, but I don't have any way of knowing for sure," she said. "You're a unique case, Eric. I've never run across an adult before with such specific, detailed memories."

"This is all more complicated than I imagined," he said. "Anything else?"

"Some people in the field believe that we travel through our lives with the same set of souls. In one life a soul might be your brother. In another, that soul could be your father or best friend. That's a little different than how we usually think of soulmates, but that's what these other souls are."

Eric took a deep breath, the air catching slightly in his throat. "I think that might be happening to me."

Carly's eyebrows lifted in intrigue. "What makes you say that?"

"When I was Tim Holt, my sister Florence...she's my mom in this life. My cousin Dickie in that life and the man I worked for when I was Cornelius Hopper, they were both my dad now. And Rachel..." His voice trailed off as he looked at Carly.

Her eyes softened. "Go on."

Eric hesitated, then met her gaze directly. "When I was out west, in Colorado, I think you were Rachel."

The silence between them was thick and charged. Carly's lips parted slightly as she processed his words. She took a steadying breath, her voice almost a whisper. "I was."

Eric's heart skipped. "Was that a question or a statement?" he asked. "It sounded like a statement."

Carly smiled faintly, her expression a mix of vulnerability and certainty. "It was a statement. I was Rachel."

"How do you know?" Eric's voice was hushed, the question carrying both awe and disbelief.

"When I was a grad student in Virginia," Carly said, her tone measured and thoughtful, "I went to a hypnotist for a past-life regression. I wasn't sure if I believed past life regressions were a hoax or if they actually worked, but I was curious. During the session, I remembered growing up on a ranch out west. I married a man who worked for my father. It was a happy life, but it was short. I died in childbirth, and so did the baby." She paused, her fingers tracing the rim of her wineglass. "After you told me about your life on the ranch, I rewatched the recording of that session. The details matched." She inhaled deeply. "I'm certain, I was Rachel."

Eric leaned back in his chair, his pulse racing. "This is crazy," he said. "What are we supposed to do now?"

Carly shook her head slowly. "I'm not sure, but I'd like you to see the video so we can talk more about it."

Eric nodded in agreement. "When can I see it?"

"How about now."

Eric finished his wine and motioned to the waiter. "Check, please."

CHAPTER 30

The phone rang and Eric opened his eyes. He was disoriented, not sure where he was. Then he caught the faint scent of Carly's perfume lingering in the air, bringing back memories of the passion they had shared the previous night. He rolled over and saw her lying next to him.

The phone rang again and he snatched it off the nightstand. It was Johan.

"The interview you did with Brady Collins came out in the *Indianapolis Star* over the weekend," Johan said. "The stuff about you living past lives has caused quite a stir. A group from some place called the Gipson Branch Evangelical Church in Oklahoma has gone down to Austin and they're protesting in front of FeeGo's headquarters."

FeeGo Streaming Service was Eric's new sponsor with Hardy-Butler Racing. He hadn't even gotten into one of their cars yet and his memories were already causing problems.

"Oh crap," Eric said, running a hand through his hair. The tangled mess mirrored the growing sense of unease knotting in his stomach. "We didn't even talk all that much about my memories. I need to call Kevin to see if this is going to be a problem."

He hung up with Johan and thought about what he should say to Kevin. His fingers lingered on the phone, hesitating, as a wave of dread surged through him.

"Is everything alright?" Carly asked. Her dark hair cascaded over the pillow, and her voice was soft with the residue of sleep. Seeing her lying there next to him made him self-conscious. He was in bed, naked, with this woman he barely knew. Then he remembered that he was also in bed with Rachel, a woman he had once intimately known in another life. The stew of emotions was confusing, his thoughts colliding in a haze of uncertainty and familiarity.

Carly's dark eyes searched his face. She looked beautiful lying there, her features relaxed, though her gaze hinted at concern. The soft morning light filtering through her bedroom window illuminated her skin, giving her an ethereal quality.

"Yeah, everything's fine," he said. "Well, maybe it's fine. My memories are causing problems for my sponsors."

He dialed Kevin's number.

"I guess you've heard," Kevin said. "There's nothing to be done at this point. I just got off the phone with Dennis Graham, the CEO of FeeGo. He says it's not much of a protest. There are fifteen or twenty people milling about in front of his building, and no one is paying attention to them."

"He's not upset?" Eric asked.

"Doesn't seem to be. In fact, he said he thinks any publicity from the protest will lead to more subscribers."

Eric laughed, a short burst of relief breaking the tension. "It would be nice if something positive came from these memories of mine."

"What protests?" Carly asked when Eric ended his call with Kevin. She sat up slightly, the sheet slipping down to reveal her bare shoulders.

"That interview I told you about with the *Indianapolis Star*. Seems some church group in Oklahoma caught wind of it and they're not too happy. They went down to Texas to protest in front of my sponsor's business."

"Is it the Gipson Branch Church?"

"Yeah," Eric said, surprised. "How did you know?"

Carly turned toward Eric and propped her head on the hand of her bent arm. "They don't like talk of reincarnation. It goes against their beliefs, and they will go anywhere, anytime to protest."

"You've dealt with them before?"

"When I was in school in Virginia, they came out and protested a research paper I co-authored. They do their best to create chaos and make things uncomfortable for the people they are protesting against, but honestly, not much came of it."

"I hope that's the case this time." Eric turned his attention to his phone. "I have to call my manager to let him know what I found out." He dialed Johan's number.

"Did you talk to Kevin?" Johan asked.

Eric told Johan about his conversation with Kevin and about what Dennis had said. "Sounds like it's not anything to worry about."

"I hope you're right," Johan said. "I saw a story on the news about the protest and they made it seem like it was a pretty big deal. They also said that some Catholic priest named Blaine McMichael is upset about the story. He writes a column for a Catholic website and has a podcast. He apparently did an emergency episode to complain about you."

"Let's hope this blows over. Dennis may not care about the protests now, but if more people join in like that priest, it could blow up."

When Eric hung up, Carly asked, "Blaine McMichael?" Her tone carried an edge that made Eric sit up straighter.

"I guess you know all the players."

"Father McMichael is another one who doesn't like reincarnation. The thing with him is that he doesn't understand the subject at all. He makes silly arguments that sound good to the uneducated, but every argument he makes is an admission of what he doesn't know."

Carly sat up in bed, the sheet covering her from the waist down, but exposing her breasts. She was obviously upset at the thought of Father McMichael, and her anger seemed to mute her modesty. She scrolled on her phone and began reading to Eric from McMichael's website.

"Reincarnation makes absolutely no sense. There are dozens of arguments to show how ridiculous it is, but one of my favorites involves simple math." Carly continued reading. *"Those that believe in reincarnation claim that we live over and over again, going from one life to another. This*

presupposes that there are a set number of souls and God isn't making any new ones. But if that is the case, how do believers in reincarnation account for the worldwide explosion in the population? They don't because they can't."

Carly put her phone down and suddenly realized she was topless. She reached over the side of the bed and grabbed her top from the previous night. She slipped it on and continued talking about the priest's argument.

"That's such a silly, simplistic argument, yet people buy what he's selling."

"How *do* you explain the population growth?" Eric asked, genuinely curious now. The logic had never crossed his mind.

Carly narrowed her eyes. "That's the wrong question," she said. "The more interesting question is, why would this priest want his followers to think that having a belief in reincarnation also means you believe the number of souls is limited?

"It's not?" he asked.

"No, it's not." There was an edge to her voice. She caught herself and let out a sigh. "I'm sorry. I forget this is all new to you." She sat up again and adjusted herself, so she was sitting cross-legged, facing Eric. "I don't know if there is a set number of souls or if God is making new ones. And neither does Father McMichael. We have no way of knowing. It could be that the number of souls is limited, and we are each living multiple lives at the same time, or maybe new souls are being created all the time. It's not an important question, but McMichael seems to think he's got it all figured out. And if you don't think too hard about it, what he says makes sense."

Eric admired her passion for and knowledge of the subject. He leaned forward and gave her a gentle kiss. "I'm glad I'm on your side of the debate."

CHAPTER 31

In the video, Carly was lying on a couch, her posture stiff. Across the room sat an older woman with long, gray hair tied loosely at the nape of her neck. She exuded a calming presence, her voice low and steady, like a distant lullaby. A single lamp cast a warm golden light that pooled around them in the dim room, making the shadows dance softly on the walls.

The woman began speaking, her words deliberate. "I want you to relax, Carly. Hypnosis is nothing more than a state of deep relaxation. You are always in control. If you want, you can open your eyes at any time."

Carly's breathing slowed, her chest rising and falling in a rhythmic pattern. For fifteen or twenty minutes, the hypnotist guided her, the hypnotist's voice weaving through the silence, a thread pulling Carly deeper into herself. Then came the countdown.

"I'm going to count backwards," the woman said. "With each number, you will move deeper into a relaxed state. And as you relax, you will allow your mind to drift—further and further back in time." Her tone was soft, her cadence melodic.

Eric watched the video beside Carly on the couch and felt an odd tension building in his chest. It was surreal to see her like this, young, open, and vulnerable in a way he had not seen her before.

"Five. Your mind is calm and at peace."

"Four. Let your thoughts drift back, just a little at first, then more and more."

"Three. Go beyond your birth in this life to a time before."

"Two. Go to a life that feels important or significant."

"One. Tell me who you are, where you are, and what you see."

There was only silence. Carly lay completely still, her face unreadable. Eric leaned forward unconsciously, waiting for her to speak. When she didn't, he considered making a joke about her falling asleep, but he kept it to himself. Finally, she spoke.

"My name is Rachel. I live on a ranch with my father. I'm making dinner for him and two other men." Her voice was lighter, almost childlike, as if it belonged to someone else entirely. And her accent had all but vanished.

The hypnotist's face remained impassive, her tone measured. "Who are the other men?"

Carly hesitated, her lips parting slightly. "They work for my father. Buck is the older one. He's been with us for years. Cole is the younger one. He's…" She paused, her voice trembling slightly before she continued. "He's strong and kind. He helps with the cattle."

Eric's stomach tightened. Cole. The name reverberated in his mind, like a tuning fork striking the core of his being.

"I'm going to move you forward to an important day in your life," the hypnotist said. "What do you see?"

Carly shifted slightly on the couch, her expression softening into one of quiet joy. "We're on the front porch of my father's house," she said. "I'm wearing a white dress I made myself. Cole is standing next to me in a starched white shirt. His usually unruly hair is combed. He's not wearing his hat. We're getting married."

"You're marrying Cole?" the hypnotist asked.

"Yes, I'm marrying Cole."

"Does your father approve of the marriage?

"Oh yes, he likes Cole very much," Carly said. "He's happy for us."

"How are you feeling?"

A smile crept onto Carly's face. "Happy," she said. "I love Cole very much. I'm looking forward to being his wife."

Eric felt an ache deep in his chest. He wanted to reach into the screen, to hold her, to tell her that Cole loved her too.

"Move forward again," the hypnotist prompted. "Go to the end of your life. What do you see?"

Carly began to shift uncomfortably on the couch, a look of anguish spreading across her face. "Oh God," she said, whispering at first, her voice rising as she described the scene. "I'm having a baby, but something is wrong. There's so much blood. I'm dying…" Her voice cracked, trembling with fear.

The hypnotist leaned forward. "Carly, I want you to separate yourself from this experience. Be an observer, not a participant. You are safe. Tell me what you see without feeling the pain."

Carly's body stilled, her face smoothing into a detached calm. "I see myself in bed. The midwife is trying to turn the baby, but it's breech. It's not working. There's nothing she can do."

She fell silent again, and Eric felt tears pricking the corners of his eyes.

"Go on," the hypnotist said gently.

"The pain stopped," Carly said, her voice distant. "I'm above my body now, looking down. I see Cole outside with my father. They look worried. I keep rising. I see the whole ranch. I loved my life on that ranch. I loved Cole." She paused. "And then it's all gone."

The screen went dark, and the silence in Carly's apartment was deafening. Eric realized he was crying. He wiped his eyes with the back of his hand, but the tears kept coming.

Carly reached out and placed her hand on his. "That was us," she said softly. "Cole and Rachel."

Eric turned to her, his eyes glassy. He pulled her into his arms, the weight of it all pressing down on him—the love, the loss, the inescapable bond they seemed destined to share. For the first time, he didn't fight the truth of his memories. He didn't know if reincarnation was real, but he did know this: in another time, in another life, he and Carly had been Cole and Rachel. They had been in love. They had been husband and wife.

The next morning, the sunlight streamed through Carly's kitchen window, casting a warm glow over the small, tidy space. Eric sat across the table from Carly, a bowl of strawberries between them. Carly's hair was tied loosely, and she wore an oversized sweater that made her look impossibly cozy.

"When we first met and I told you my story, did you know then that you were Rachel and I was Cole?" Eric picked a strawberry from the bowl and rolled it between his fingers.

Carly dipped a strawberry in sugar and took a thoughtful bite. "Not for sure," she said. "There were similarities to our stories—especially the names—but what were the odds? Then, you told me about Rachel wearing different colored ribbons in her hair, and I knew it had to be more than coincident."

"Why didn't you say anything?"

Carly took another bite of strawberry. A trickle of juice slid onto her chin and she wiped it with a napkin. "I reasoned that if I remembered who we were, you would remember me too. Plus, you had a girlfriend." She gave him a wry smile.

Eric chuckled softly. "Yes, my girlfriend."

Carly laughed, the sound light and unguarded. "I can't believe I told you it would be best if you didn't bring her back to the office."

"To your credit, you were diplomatic about it."

Carly's smile widened. "I can't help it. I'm British."

Eric leaned back in his chair, his expression growing serious. "So, what does this mean for us?"

Carly sighed and her gaze softened. "It means whatever you want it to mean," she said. "Just because we were together in another life doesn't mean we're required to be together in this one. Last night can be the entirety of our relationship, or it can be the start of it."

"I think I'd like it to be the start."

"Me too," Carly said. "But we need to be careful. Lingering feelings from a past life shouldn't be confused with what we feel now. This is a new life. A different life. Despite our memories, we both need to make sure we're living in the present."

Eric reached across the table, taking her hand in his. "I'm very much in the present when I say I think we should go back to bed."

Carly picked up a strawberry and fed it to him, her eyes sparkling with mischief. "I like the way you think."

CHAPTER 32

The hostess showed them to their table, a cozy spot near a wide window that bathed the room in soft, natural light. The soft euphony of Sunday brunch surrounded them—the clinking of silverware against plates, bursts of laughter, and the mellow notes of a jazz trio playing in the corner across the room.

Connie ordered a mimosa as soon as she was seated. Eric opted for water, though he hesitated for a moment as the waitress scribbled down their drink order.

"Don't you think it's strange that society frowns on people drinking too early in the day, but if you go to brunch, all bets are off?" he asked. "In fact, you're almost expected to have a mimosa or a bloody Mary."

Connie raised an eyebrow and gave him a wry smile. "Honestly, I've never thought about it."

"Maybe you should."

"Or maybe you should stop thinking about it and order one for yourself." Her teasing tone made them both laugh.

The waitress returned with Connie's mimosa, its orange hue glinting in the sunlight. She placed Eric's water in front of him.

Eric lifted his drink and stared at it forlornly. "I've had a change of heart," he said to the waitress. "I'd like a mimosa too."

Connie chuckled. "Now you're talking."

As the waitress walked away, Connie took a sip of her drink, the condensation from the glass dampening her fingers.

"Aren't you even going to wait for me?" Eric asked, feigning indignation.

"You'll catch up." She winked, her playful grin softening the edges of her words. "So, I'm anxious to hear about what Dr. Pellegrino found out about your memories."

Eric leaned back in his chair, folding his arms across his chest. "There's a lot to tell. Let's start one life ago. I was a home builder for a while in Chicago, then moved to Wisconsin and became a handyman and fishing guide."

Connie tilted her head, her expression caught between curiosity and disbelief. "Were you married?"

"No, I never got married. I was too busy sleeping with my business partner's wife and getting drunk."

Connie nearly choked on her mimosa. "Is that true?" she asked.

"It is." A rueful smile tugged at his lips. "I'm afraid I wasn't a very good person in that life."

She brushed aside his self-deprecation with a wave of her hand. "What else can you tell me about…what was your name?"

"Ted."

"What else can you tell me about Ted?"

Eric sighed, drumming his fingers lightly on the table. "I died young," he said. "I was just forty-one. I drowned in a lake up in Rhinelander, Wisconsin in 1991."

Connie frowned, her lips tightening into a thin line. "I wonder if that's why you don't like to swim now."

Eric sat back, the observation landing with surprising weight. "I never thought of that," he said. "All my life, I've avoided the water, but I never understood why."

"When you were a young boy—I think you were five—we took you for swimming lessons. You cried the whole time and begged us not to take you back."

Eric chuckled softly, a note of melancholy threading through his laughter. "I never did learn to swim very well."

Connie leaned forward, her eyes sharp with curiosity. "Okay, that's not a very happy life. What about the one before that?"

"I'm afraid that wasn't much happier," he said, his tone growing somber. "That's the life when you were Florence."

The waitress returned with Eric's mimosa. He took a long drink, savoring the citrusy sweetness, then compared his glass to Connie's. "There, now we're even."

"Don't worry about that," she said. "Tell me about Florence."

Eric nodded, his gaze distant as if peering into the past. "You were my sister. I was a mistake. Our parents were older and didn't plan on having me. Because you were significantly older, you tended to take care of me more than our parents. We were very close."

Connie's smile softened, a wistful expression settling on her face. "What was your name? Where did we live? Did we have any other brothers or sisters?"

"You're full of questions, aren't you?" Eric teased. "My name was Tim Holt. You were Florence Holt. We lived in Canada. I don't remember any other brothers or sisters, but we did have a cousin who was around all the time. His name was Dickie, and he was a bully. He used to pick on me, and you tried to protect me from him."

Connie's brow furrowed. "That's not good. What happened to Dickie?"

Eric's expression shifted, a flicker of astonishment crossing his face. "Wait a minute," he said. "You're accepting all this as if it's the truth? You believe my story about Ted and this one about Tim?"

"I assume they're true," she said. "You're remembering them, right?"

"I am. What I'm asking is, do you really believe my memories are from past lives?"

Connie paused, her eyes narrowing thoughtfully. "Yeah, I guess I do," she said. "Tell me more."

Eric's lips pressed into a thin line. "You might not like this next part."

Her eyes widened. "Now I really want to know."

Eric nodded slowly, as if bracing himself. "Dad was Dickie."

The words hung in the air for a moment.

Connie shook her head. "I don't know what you mean."

Eric repeated himself, this time more slowly. "Dad. Was. Dickie."

Connie's expression shifted from confusion to shock. "Your dad? He was there with us?" she asked. "How do you know?"

"The same way I know that you were Florence," Eric said. "I recognize you both from my memories. In another life, one in England, I worked for Dad. I was his butler."

Connie's eyes searched his face, her expression a mix of disbelief and fascination. "Was I in any of your other lives?"

Eric shook his head. "I don't think so. Not that I remember."

Connie's gaze dropped to her mimosa. She swirled the liquid absent-mindedly. "Why was he in two of your past lives and I was only in one?"

Eric grinned. "Are you jealous?"

"Maybe I am." Her tone had a hint of humor, but her eyes were serious. "I just never considered that your father would be in any of your past lives."

"If it makes you feel better, he wasn't very nice to me in either of those lives."

"That doesn't make me feel better," she said. She waved the thought away. "Enough about him. Tell me more about our lives in Canada."

"There's not a lot more to tell. When I got out of high school, I joined the military. I was in the Canadian Army and was sent to Europe for the D-Day invasion. I died in 1945 in the Netherlands. I drowned in that life too, before I even reached the beach."

Connie's breath caught, her hand covering her mouth. "You died? You were so young."

Eric chuckled, trying to lighten the mood. "You didn't think I lived forever, did you? I died and came back as Ted Humphrey in Chicago."

"Don't laugh," she said. "I know you didn't live forever, but I still find it upsetting. You were my brother. Did Dr. Pellegrino tell you anything else?"

Eric leaned back and crossed his legs. "Funny you should ask," he said. "Do you remember when I was in the hospital, and I told you about Rachel?"

Connie's eyes lit with recognition. "She was your wife in Colorado."

"That's right," he said. "A couple days ago, I learned that Carly—Dr. Pellegrino—was Rachel."

Connie's jaw dropped. "Dr. Pellegrino was Rachel?" she asked. "How can you be sure?"

Eric finished his mimosa, savoring the last sip before responding. "Just like with you, I remembered her. Not right away, but the more I was around her, the more I came to realize that she was Rachel. At dinner the other night, I told her about it, and she said that she already knew."

"How could she know?" Her voice was skeptical but curious.

"Several years ago, when she was going to school in Virginia, she underwent a hypnotic regression. She remembered being in Colorado and being married to someone named Cole. When I told her about Rachel, it matched what she remembered during the regression. She had a video of the session, and she showed it to me. There's no doubt in my mind, she's Rachel."

"Oh my gosh. That's amazing," Connie said. "And wonderful. And romantic."

Eric smiled. "It is kind of romantic, isn't it?"

"So, what now?" Connie asked, leaning forward eagerly.

"What do you mean?"

"Are you going to date her? I mean, is that even appropriate?"

"It is appropriate, and I'm already dating her."

Connie's face lit up with genuine joy. "Eric, that's wonderful," she said, her voice brimming with warmth. "You and Dr. Pellegrino."

Eric chuckled. "You should probably call her Carly."

She nodded, her smile widening. "You and Carly."

CHAPTER 33

The snow started around noon on New Year's Day and continued until late into the evening, blanketing the city in a thick, quiet stillness. Eric hadn't intended to spend the night at Carly's, but the worsening weather had made travel dangerous. Secretly, he was glad for the excuse. The thought of spending an unhurried evening with her felt like a gift wrapped in soft snowfall.

Carly's apartment was warm and inviting, filled with the scent of cinnamon candles and the faint aroma of the pizza they had shared earlier that evening. They lounged on the couch like an old married couple, her feet tucked under a knitted blanket and his socked feet propped on the coffee table. They watched TV, snacked on salty chips and spicy salsa, and read to each other. Carly read aloud from a book by her mentor, Brian Stevens, which led to a discussion about the paper Carly had written about Eric's memories.

"When is your paper about me going to be published?" he asked.

"Any day now," she said. "It's scheduled for publication this month."

"I can't wait. I'm looking forward to reading it."

She set her book down and smiled. "You don't have to wait," she said. "I have a copy right here." She reached for her laptop, navigated to the file, and handed it to Eric.

He settled the computer on his lap and began to read, his brow furrowing in concentration. Carly rose from the couch and padded into the kitchen. "Do you want some ice cream?" she called over her shoulder.

"Sure, that sounds great," Eric said without looking up.

Carly dished up two bowls of French vanilla ice cream and brought them back to the living room. She placed Eric's bowl on the coffee table, the cold ceramic creating a faint circle of condensation on the polished wood. He didn't touch it, too engrossed in the words glowing on the laptop screen. When he finished reading, the ice cream had begun to melt, pooling into creamy rivulets along the edges of the bowl.

"Why didn't you write about when we were together as Cole and Rachel?" he asked.

Carly tucked her legs beneath her, her bowl balanced on her lap. "Eat your ice cream before it's completely melted." She took a spoonful of ice cream, then set the bowl on the table.

"The paper is only about your life in Chicago and Rhinelander. That's the most recent one and the one with the most documentation. There was enough material from that life to fill an entire article. But I also didn't want to write anything about us being a couple in a previous life. I didn't want to include any personal stuff. It could distract from my research."

Eric took a bite of the softened ice cream and let the cool sweetness linger on his tongue. "I think I prefer ice cream that's half melted."

"I'll put it in the microwave for you next time."

"I appreciate that." He laughed, taking another spoonful of the ice cream. "I also appreciate you not using my name in the article. I'm not embarrassed about my memories, but it's probably best to separate my career from those memories."

Carly had been meticulous in maintaining Eric's anonymity. In the paper, she'd used a pseudonym and described his accident in broad terms, omitting any mention of racing or the Indianapolis Motor Speedway.

Eric stirred his ice cream thoughtfully. "I didn't realize you spoke to Bridget Driggins about her affair with Ted."

"She confirmed the affair and said she never talked to Driggins after he left her, but she didn't have much else to add," Carly said. "She's an old woman now, and I don't think she's particularly proud of how she lived her life when she was younger."

Eric nodded, his gaze dropping to the bowl in his hands. "Do you really think people would doubt your research if they knew that we were together as Cole and Rachel?"

Carly sighed, brushing a strand of hair from her face. "I'm afraid they would. There are a lot of charlatans out there trying to make money by making up stories. What we do is impossible to prove conclusively, so it attracts unsavory characters who see creating hoaxes as a way to earn a living. For those of us doing legitimate work, we can't give anyone a reason to doubt us."

"That makes sense." He took the final bite of his ice cream and held the empty bowl in both hands. "Are you going to write more about my memories?"

A smile spread across Carly's face. "Not for another academic journal, but I just signed a contract with a publisher to expand the paper into a book."

"A book? Really?" Eric's eyebrows shot up. "Are you going to talk more about my other lives in the book?"

Carly nodded, a hint of excitement in her expression. "I think so. A book gives me the space to write about all your lives. And because it'll be more mainstream, the level of proof doesn't have to be as high as in an academic publication. This could be a chance to share my research with a much wider audience and to potentially make reincarnation a more accepted part of the culture."

Eric congratulated her, his words sincere but laced with concern. A paper in an obscure academic journal was one thing; a book—especially if it gained traction and popularity—was another. The thought of his memories becoming public knowledge to a wider audience unsettled him. But for now, he wanted to savor the moment.

"Can I ask you a serious question?" Eric's tone grew soft, his eyes searching Carly's.

Carly turned to face him fully, her expression open and curious. "Of course."

"Do you have any more ice cream?"

CHAPTER 34

The streets of St. Petersburg were alive with energy, a pulsating mix of celebration and chaos as fans swarmed the paddock. The air was thick with the mingling scents of fuel, rubber, and sea breeze. The sun dipped low, casting long shadows across the bustling scene. Eric weaved through the crowd, his sweat-soaked race suit clinging to his body as he headed toward the Hardy-Butler Racing hauler to change into fresh clothes.

The car Hardy-Butler provided was everything Eric could have hoped for—fast, responsive, and a joy to drive. He had qualified seventh on the grid, and after a smart, mistake-free race, he crossed the finish line in fifth place. But it wasn't the top five finish that mattered most. For the first time in ten months, he felt like himself again. Back in the car, driving on the edge, he was no longer defined by the whispers about his strange memories or the doubts surrounding his return. He was once again a race car driver.

As he neared the team's hauler, the familiar roar of the crowd softened, replaced by the strum of conversations and the clinking of tools being packed away. He allowed himself a moment to savor the satisfaction of the day. Then a voice cut through the din, stopping him in his tracks.

"Hey, Eric! Eric!"

He turned, his eyes narrowing as they landed on the man approaching him. It took a moment for recognition to dawn, and when it did, his stomach tightened. Martin Simms, his father, stood before him, looking older but still bearing the same sharp features Eric had inherited.

"Hello, son."

Eric's jaw dropped, and he struggled to find words. "Dad? What are you doing here?"

Martin didn't offer his hand or attempt an embrace. "I came to see you race. Why else would I be here?"

He thought of his father's absence throughout much of his life, his drunken tirades, the weight of his disapproval. And now, here he was, showing up unannounced, as if the past decade of estrangement could be erased with a casual "hello."

"You did great today," Martin said. "Just great." His words fit the moment, but his mannerisms were sheepish.

"Yeah, thanks." Eric's tone was clipped. His gaze darted around in search of an escape but didn't see one he could take that wouldn't make the already awkward situation even more so.

Martin had aged noticeably. His hair was thinner, streaked with gray, and his frame was leaner than Eric remembered. But his eyes still held that piercing quality, the same intensity that had always unsettled Eric as a child. Yet there was something different now—a vulnerability that softened his father's usually rigid demeanor.

"I was hoping I could talk to you about this past life stuff I've been hearing about," Martin said, glancing at the people streaming by.

"What do you want to know?" His voice was cold, uninterested.

"I called your mom a couple weeks ago to see how you were doing," Martin said, shifting from foot to foot uncomfortably. "She told me about your memories and mentioned I was part of them. She wouldn't go into specifics but said I showed up in some of your past lives."

Eric's jaw tightened. He debated how much, if anything, he should share. Finally, he decided on a bare-bones explanation. "You showed up in a couple of my memories," he said. "Once in England, where I worked for you, and once in Canada, where you were my cousin."

Martin waited for Eric to continue, then realized he was done speaking. He tilted his head, his eyes searching Eric's "What can you tell me about these people?" He waved his hand vaguely. "You know, these other versions of me."

Eric's patience was already wearing thin. "Mom said you didn't believe in reincarnation. Why are you even interested?" Eric didn't intend for his voice to sound so chilly, but he couldn't help it.

Martin sighed, looking down at his feet before meeting Eric's gaze. "I used to think reincarnation was nonsense," he said. "A load of crap. But as I've gotten older, I've started to question a lot of things I used to be absolutely sure about."

Eric raised an eyebrow. The man who had once been so dogmatic, so certain of his own infallibility, was now admitting doubt. It was almost enough to soften Eric's resolve. Almost.

"You weren't a very nice guy in either life," Eric said. "In England, I was your butler, and you used to beat me with a cane when you were drunk. When I got tuberculosis, you sent me away to a sanitorium and never saw me again."

Martin's face paled. "Was I just as bad in Canada?"

"Maybe worse," Eric said. "You bullied me relentlessly. I joined the army just to get away from you, and I ended up dying in Europe during World War II."

For a moment, Martin looked like he'd been punched in the gut. He opened his mouth to speak but hesitated a beat. "I guess I wasn't much better in this life," he said quietly.

Eric's first instinct was to tell his father he wasn't all bad, to offer some shred of absolution. But he stopped himself. His father had made his choices, and it wasn't Eric's responsibility to ease his guilt. Still, watching the older man shrink under the weight of his own failings stirred an uncomfortable mix of pity and resentment in Eric's chest.

Eric felt the weight of the dissonance he was experiencing. On the one hand, his father had chosen to be distant, uninvolved in his life. On the other, Eric yearned to understand why his father was the way he was; why he had been that way through different lives.

"It was good seeing you, Eric," Martin said. "Congratulations on a great race." Then he turned and disappeared into the crowd.

Eric stood watching his father's retreating figure. The encounter left him feeling raw, a knot of conflicting emotions tightening in his gut. He wanted to forget it, to push it aside and focus on the day's triumphs. But the dissonance lingered, a dull ache that refused to be ignored.

He made his way to the hauler, changed out of his race suit, and pulled on a pair of jeans and a T-shirt. He'd shower back at the motorhome. For now, he just wanted to find Carly and celebrate with a beer.

As he stepped outside, he nearly collided with Michelle.

"Eric. Hi," she said, her voice tinged with surprise.

"Hi, Michelle." He forced a polite smile. "How are you?"

"I'm good," she said, her gaze flickering uncertainly. "Congratulations on the race today."

"Thanks."

An awkward silence stretched between them. Eric didn't want to prolong the interaction but couldn't think of a way to end it without seeming rude.

"You know, we never really had the opportunity to talk about our breakup." Michelle twirled a strand of hair around her finger. "There are things I'd like to talk to you about."

Eric knew Michelle well enough to know that she was trying to butter him up for something. He wasn't sure if she wanted to get back together or if she wanted to tell him off, but in either case, he wasn't interested. "That's probably not a good idea, Michelle," he said. "I think it's best to leave well enough alone."

Michelle hesitated, her expression shifting from hopeful to defensive. "But I think…"

Before she could finish, Carly slid in next to Eric, slipping her arm around his waist and kissing his cheek. "Great race, love."

Turning to Michelle, Carly extended her hand. "Oh, hi. It's Michelle, isn't it?"

Michelle blinked, clearly caught off guard. She quickly shook Carly's hand. "I have to go," she said abruptly. "Nice seeing you, Eric." Without another word, she hurried away.

"I hope I didn't interrupt anything," Carly said, a mischievous smile playing on her lips.

"Not at all," Eric said, pulling her closer. "You saved me. Let's get a drink."

CHAPTER 35

Eric's phone buzzed against the counter, cutting through the stillness of his quiet morning. He glanced at the screen, surprised to see Carly's name. They'd settled into a rhythm in their relationship—easy, steady, full of daily calls and regular dinners. But Carly rarely called during work hours, her nine-to-five keeping her busy with patients and research. He swiped to answer, curiosity blooming alongside a flicker of concern.

"To what do I owe this pleasure?" he asked.

"Do you remember those protesters down in Texas?" she asked. "The ones from Gipson Branch Church?" Carly's question carried an undercurrent of tension.

Eric's brow furrowed. "The ones protesting FeeGo? Yeah, I remember. Why?"

"They're here."

He blinked, the weight of her words sinking in. "Here? As in Indianapolis?"

"Here, as in outside my office." Carly's tone was more amused than alarmed, like protesters descending on her workplace was just another Tuesday.

Eric's pulse quickened. "What are they doing at your office?"

"Protesting," she said. "Apparently, my paper in *Parapsychology Review* didn't sit well with them."

He exhaled sharply. "How many people are we talking about?"

"Fifty or sixty at the moment," Carly said. "Father McMichael just joined them, complete with his loyal flock of followers. They have signs, chants, the whole production. It's all very impressive."

Eric's lips twitched, wanting to smile, yet failing to see the humor in the situation. "You sound like you're enjoying this."

"Oh, I'm not running outside to join them, if that's what you mean. But it's so…theatrical."

"Theatrical?" he asked. "Carly, this sounds serious. Maybe you should leave."

Her voice sharpened with resolve. "Leave? Absolutely not. I'm not going to let them scare me off."

Eric sighed, shaking his head at her stubbornness. "If you're not leaving, then I'm coming over."

She laughed softly, the sound easing the knot in his chest. "That would be brilliant. I'd love to see you. Maybe we can order out for lunch."

"You're braver than I am," he said, reaching for his jacket.

"That, coming from a man who drives at over two hundred miles an hour?"

"That's not bravery," he said. "That's stupidity. I'll be there in ten minutes."

When Eric pulled into the parking lot behind Carly's office, the scale of the protest hit him. The crowd spilled across the front lawn onto the sidewalk and into the street, a sea of signs waving in the spring breeze. Police officers loitered nearby, ensuring the demonstrators didn't block traffic or damage property. As he drove past, several protesters yelled and pointed at his car, their words drowned out by the car radio.

The scene confused him. How had his memories led to this? He didn't understand why church groups, people who presumably worshipped the same God as he did were so upset by his memories and Carly's article about them. And what was with the anti-abortion signs? What did any of this have to do with abortion?

He rushed from his car into the building where Carly greeted him with a quick, tight hug, one that lingered just long enough to betray her nerves. Her outward composure didn't fool him; she was rattled, even if she refused to show it.

"I think you might have undercounted the number of protesters," Eric said, glancing toward the window.

"A few more must have arrived since we talked." Carly maintained her amused tone, but the way she held herself, shoulders slightly hunched, hinted at the tension she was carrying.

"Why the anti-abortion signs?" Eric gestured toward the window.

Carly's lips pressed into a thin line. "I think it's about a paper I co-authored back in Virginia when I was a grad student."

"About abortion?"

"Not exactly." She motioned for Eric to follow her, and they went into her office. "The paper was about some kids we interviewed in India. Several of them remembered the moment they entered their body. For all of them, it was at the moment of birth."

"Right. You've told me about that before," Eric said, leaning against her desk. "But I still don't get the connection to abortion."

"Neither did we, at first," Carly said. "Apparently, some pro-life groups latched onto the findings, claiming we were pushing a pro-choice agenda."

Eric's eyes lit with understanding. "Because if the soul doesn't enter the body until birth, it undermines the idea that life begins at conception? And if the soul isn't present until birth, abortion before then isn't nearly as serious?"

"Exactly." Carly folded her arms, leaning against the edge of her desk. "But that wasn't our argument. None of us were thinking about abortion when we wrote that paper. It was purely about the phenomenon of past-life memories."

Eric nodded, absorbing her words. "Makes sense. But why stay here? Why not go somewhere safe?"

Her eyes flashed with defiance. "Because this is my office. My work. I'm not going to let them intimidate me."

He tilted his head, a faint smile tugging at his lips. "Are you actually getting any work done?"

"Not a chance," Carly said, the corner of her mouth quirking up.

"And yet you stay."

"Stubborn, isn't it?" She shrugged and revealed a sly smile.

Eric chuckled, shaking his head. "Let me take you out of here" he said. "We'll get lunch."

Her smile softened, and she reached for his hand. "I'll allow it, but only if you're buying."

He squeezed her hand gently. "Deal."

CHAPTER 36

Eric chuckled softly as Carly handed the menu back to the waitress and ordered a glass of wine. The café around them was a quaint, inviting space, its walls adorned with rustic farm memorabilia—aged wagon wheels, rusted milk churns, and black-and-white photographs of somber-faced farmers. A verdant collection of plants hung from macramé holders, their leaves spilling gracefully toward the exposed brick walls. Only a few tables were occupied, the café cozy and quiet.

"What?" Carly asked, arching a playful eyebrow as she caught Eric's amused expression.

"Kind of early for wine, isn't it?" He leaned back in his chair. "We haven't even made it to noon."

"I need it today," she said, brushing her hair behind one ear with a flourish of mock drama. "And I don't need any commentary from you."

Eric grinned, holding up his hands in faux surrender. "No commentary, I promise. Just making sure you know what time it is."

Carly stuck out her tongue at him, the gesture so endearingly juvenile that Eric couldn't help but laugh.

"Seriously, though, are you feeling more relaxed now that we're away from your office?" he asked. "Those protesters would've rattled anyone."

Carly exhaled, her shoulders easing as she settled deeper into her chair. "I'll feel more relaxed once that wine gets here," she said, flashing a quick smile that didn't entirely mask the lingering tension in her voice.

The waitress returned with their drinks, setting Carly's wine and Eric's water on the table in front of them. Carly wasted no time, taking a generous sip of the dark liquid and letting out a small sigh of satisfaction.

"I may need a couple more of these," she said, setting the glass down with care.

Eric leaned forward, his elbows resting on the table. "Do you think this whole protest thing will blow over soon?"

Carly swirled the wine in her glass thoughtfully. "I doubt they'll stay long," she said. "These groups thrive on outrage. Give it a day or two, and they'll find some new grievance to get incensed over. They'll pack up their traveling circus and head down the road."

Eric chuckled at her choice of words, but Carly's expression turned serious. "What worries me isn't the protests themselves, it's the potential fallout. These kinds of public spectacles can scare off donors."

"Donors?" Eric leaned in closer.

Carly nodded, her fingers tracing the edge of her glass. "One of my biggest responsibilities as director of the Center is keeping us funded," she said. "When Dr. Rasmussen started the Center, we had steady donors who covered everything—salaries, travel, research expenses. But when he retired, some of that funding dried up. Every year, it's been harder to keep the lights on."

Eric nodded, taking a sip of his water.

"And protests like this don't help," she said. "They make potential donors wary of being associated with anything remotely controversial. They support our work, but they don't want to be associated with anything that leads to protests, especially from church groups."

Eric frowned as he absorbed her words. "How bad is it?"

Her eyes flicked to his, her calm exterior cracking slightly. "Bad. We're down to just me and Rose now, and she's only part-time. If I can't raise $50,000 in the next few months…" She raised her eyebrows and trailed off, taking another sip of her wine.

"What happens if you can't?" he asked.

Carly exhaled sharply, her shoulders sagging. "Worst case? I have to let Rose go and sell the building. I don't even know if the Center could survive after that."

Eric reached across the table, his hand covering hers. "You'll find a way," he said. "You're too damn stubborn to let it fail."

Her lips curved into a small, grateful smile. "I hope you're right."

The waitress returned to check on them, and Carly ordered a second glass of wine. She shot Eric a mock-warning look before he could comment, and he chuckled, raising his water glass in a silent toast.

After lunch, they went back to Carly's apartment. As they walked from the car through the cool spring air, Carly held on to Eric's arm and leaned against him, her head briefly resting against his shoulder.

"That wine made me sleepy," she said. "Will you take a nap with me?"

He chuckled, wrapping his arm tighter around her. "I'd be honored."

Inside, Carly kicked off her boots and led him to the bedroom. The soft glow of afternoon light filtered through the sheer curtains, casting delicate patterns on the walls. They crawled into bed, the quiet intimacy of the moment wrapping around them like a warm blanket. Carly fell asleep almost instantly, her breathing steady and rhythmic. Eric lay beside her, watching her peaceful expression, his mind a tangle of thoughts.

How improbable it all was—this connection they shared, stretching through lifetimes. In Carly, he found not only a partner but a mirror to his soul, a piece of himself that had been missing for so long he hadn't even realized it was gone. He reached out, brushing a stray curl from her face and pressing a gentle kiss to her forehead.

She stirred slightly but didn't wake. Eric closed his eyes, letting the quiet wash over him.

When he woke, the light in the room was dim, the faint orange glow of sunset casting shadows on the walls. He blinked, disoriented for a moment, before realizing Carly was lying on her side, watching him.

"I love you," she said. Her voice was barely above a whisper.

Eric smiled, reaching for her. "I love you, too."

Her gaze searched his, her vulnerability catching him off guard. "Are you sure you love me? Or is it the Rachel part of me that you love?"

Eric's expression grew thoughtful as he considered her question. "I love you," he said finally. "I'm certain of that. But I love Rachel too. I can separate my life with you from my memories of Rachel, but it's harder to separate my feelings. I love the Carly that you are now and the Rachel that you were then. That love is like a thread, continuous and unbroken. I think I've loved you starting with our lives on the ranch, going through my life in Chicago, straight through to today. Not having you during those lives was like a hole in my heart. A void I could never fill. Until now."

Her lips curved into a small, tender smile. "That's a perfect answer."

"I'm glad you think so." He leaned in to kiss her gently on the lips. She returned the kiss, and it became less gentle, more demanding. He was only too happy to give into those demands.

They dressed quietly, the intimacy of the afternoon lingering between them like a shared secret, then made their way to the living room. Carly's apartment was nearly dark now, the streetlamps casting shadows across the ceiling. They settled onto the couch, the cushions soft and familiar beneath them. Carly turned on the local news. She held the remote loosely in her hand, her thumb hovering over the volume button as they waited to see if the protests had made the headlines.

It didn't take long to find out. The second story of the broadcast opened with an aerial shot of the Center for Past Life Research. The image, sharp and unwavering, revealed a throng of protesters swarming the building's exterior, their signs bobbing like restless boats in a choppy sea. Eric leaned forward, his elbows on his knees, as the sight of the crowd filled the screen.

"This must have been taken from a helicopter," Carly said. Her gaze remained fixed on the television. "I don't remember seeing one when we left."

Eric studied the footage. "It must have been shot after we were already gone," he said.

Carly clicked the volume button, the female reporter's voice filling the room.

"...in front of the Center for Past Life Research in Indianapolis. The Center is at the heart of a controversy involving a research paper written by the Center's director, Dr. Carly Pellegrino, and involving popular IndyCar driver, Eric Simms. According to the paper, after suffering head trauma in an accident while qualifying for last year's Indy 500, Simms began having unexplained memories that Pellegrino's paper contends are from previous lives he has lived."

Eric straightened, his shoulders stiffening as his name echoed through the speakers, his pulse quickening.

The reporter continued. "I asked Reverend James Raley, pastor of the Gipson Branch Evangelical Church in Oklahoma, who organized the protests, what had upset him and brought him and his congregation to Indianapolis."

The screen shifted to a close-up of Reverend Raley, his lined face framed by white hair and a meticulously trimmed beard. His wire-rimmed glasses glinted under the camera lights, giving him an air of stern authority. The chyron at the bottom of the screen read: *Reverend James Raley, Gipson Branch Evangelical Church.*

"Dr. Carly Pellegrino and Eric Simms are trying to deceive the God-fearing people of this country by convincing them that when we die, we don't go to Heaven or hell, but instead live another life here on Earth." Raley's voice was steady and forceful. "This is a ruse, and Dr. Pellegrino is a charlatan with a long history of these types of anti-Christian tricks. The Bible makes it clear that we live one life, and it is only through Jesus Christ, the son of God, that we can have eternal life in Heaven."

The screen shifted again, this time to the reporter standing beside a man in a black cassock. The white collar around his neck gleamed starkly under the camera lights. His expression was grim, his hands clasped in front of him as though he were about to deliver a sermon.

"I'm now with Father Blaine McMichael of the popular *Catholic Thought* podcast," the reporter said, turning toward the priest. "Father, what brings you and your followers out here today?"

Father McMichael's voice was sharp, his words cutting. "The director of this institution, Dr. Cathy Pellegrino, is a so-called scientist who writes propaganda in support of abortionists. She works along with the feminists and baby-killing doctors to try to convince people that abortions should be allowed on demand, up to and including after the baby is born. This is nothing but murder, plain and simple, and it's up to people like me and other right-thinking Catholics to point out these evil acts and actors."

Eric let out a low, incredulous sigh as the camera zoomed in on the reporter. "We reached out to Dr. Pellegrino for comment, but she did not return our calls. From the Center for Past Life Research in Indianapolis, I'm Brianna Hartley reporting."

The newscast shifted to a mundane story about local road construction, and Carly clicked the remote, silencing the television.

"How the hell did they know my name?" Eric asked, breaking the silence.

"How did Father McMichael get my name wrong?"

Eric managed a dry chuckle despite himself. "Yeah, I noticed that. *Cathy Pellegrino,* huh?"

Carly shrugged, her expression unreadable. "I don't know how they got your name, Eric. If I had to guess, they probably saw you at the office today and put two and two together."

He sighed, leaning back against the couch. "Of course, that article in the *IndyStar* I did after I signed with Hardy-Butler was probably a tip-off too. I didn't even think about it then."

Carly reached out, placing a hand on his arm. Her touch was grounding, though it did little to ease the knot of tension in his chest. "What do we do now?"

Chapter 37

The conference room was utilitarian, its walls lined with posters of past races and a whiteboard filled with hastily scrawled notes about car setups and sponsor obligations. Eric sat across the table from Kevin, his boss's face passive, undecipherable. Eric's stomach churned with a mixture of anticipation and resignation, the table between them like a gulf.

Kevin dialed Dennis Graham's number on the speakerphone. Eric tapped his fingers against the edge of the table, a nervous habit that betrayed his cool exterior. Kevin shot him a glance, and Eric stopped, clasping his hands together.

Dennis's assistant answered, and Kevin introduced himself and requested to speak with Dennis. They were put on hold, the tinny strains of generic on-hold music filling the silence. The melody grated on Eric's nerves, making the wait feel interminable.

"I got a copy of Carly's article in *Parapsychology Review*." Kevin leaned back in his chair, folding his arms across his chest. "It's a little highbrow and academic for me, but it's a hell of a story. Is everything she wrote true? You remembered all that stuff?"

Eric nodded, though his expression remained guarded. "Everything she wrote is from my memories, but I still don't know if it's true. It's hard to wrap my head around the idea of living past lives."

Kevin let out a low whistle. "I can understand that. It's crazy stuff, but it was a good read. They should make a movie out of that article."

Eric smirked, shaking his head. "Not sure about the movie idea, but thanks. I think."

The music stopped abruptly, and Dennis's cheerful Australian accent filled the room. "Kevin, it's good to hear from you."

"Hi, Dennis," Kevin said, leaning forward slightly. "I've got Eric here with me. We wanted to check in, see how you're feeling about the news report about the protests here in Indianapolis. The one that mentioned Eric and his past life memories."

"I'm ecstatic," Dennis said, his tone buoyant. "Checked this morning, and subscriptions in the Indianapolis market were up five percent overnight. The biggest jump in the nation. The season's only just begun, and we're already seeing a return on our investment. It's brilliant, mates."

Eric blinked, startled by Dennis's enthusiasm. He had expected frustration and anger, not glee.

"I'm happy to hear that, Dennis," Kevin said, his voice calm but edged with relief. "I was worried you might not be happy with the story."

"Oh, no, I'm thrilled," Dennis replied. "This is wonderful for us. I've got our PR people working on turning this into a national story. Eric, I hope you'll be available for any interviews we arrange. People are fascinated by your story, and because of our association, they're interested in subscribing to FeeGo. I wish we had another race tomorrow to use the car to spread the story. Soon enough, I suppose."

Kevin glanced at Eric, his eyebrows raised in silent question. Eric nodded.

"I'm sure Eric will be available for those interviews," Kevin said. "Thanks for your time, Dennis. Let us know if you need anything from us."

After they hung up, a charged silence filled the room. Kevin was the first to speak. "That went better than I expected."

Eric let out a breath he didn't realize he'd been holding. "Yeah, who would've guessed my memories would turn out to be a good thing?"

Kevin grinned, the lines around his eyes crinkling. "How do you feel about doing a bunch of interviews?"

Eric cleared his throat. "Truthfully, not crazy about it. But if it keeps Dennis happy, I'll do it."

"That's the spirit," Kevin said, clapping him on the shoulder. "Anything for the sponsor."

When Eric had left Carly's apartment that morning, his mood had been heavy, clouded by worry about the protests and the news report. Now, he was eager to see her face light up when he shared how well the conversation with Dennis had gone.

But as soon as he stepped into her apartment, he saw Carly sitting at the small dinette table, her phone pressed to her ear. Her posture was tense, her free hand gripping the edge of the table. The expression on her face a mixture of frustration and sadness.

"I understand," she said into the phone, her voice low and steady despite the strain evident in her tone. "I look forward to explaining myself. Thank you."

She hung up and let out a long, shuddering exhale. "Bloody hell."

Eric moved towards her. "What's wrong?"

Carly rubbed her temples, her elbows propped on the table. She looked up at him, her eyes glassy. "That was the editor of *Parapsychology Review*. They're concerned I didn't disclose our relationship, and they're questioning my findings. They might retract the article."

Eric's heart sank. "Why? What does our relationship have to do with your paper? How would that change anything?"

Carly exhaled deeply and gathered her thoughts. "It's an academic journal," she said. "They have incredibly high standards. The field of parapsychology is constantly under attack by skeptics, and the journal tries to avoid anything that could be seen as biased or unethical. To them, our relationship might make the findings look suspicious, like we were collaborating to fabricate the story."

"Would it help if I talked to them? Told them this is real?"

Carly gave him a small, sad smile. "Thank you, but I'm afraid it wouldn't make a difference," she said. "They've scheduled a Zoom meeting with their review board tomorrow so I can explain myself. Then they'll decide whether or not to retract the paper."

"But they've already published it. How can they retract it?"

"They'd issue a formal retraction," Carly said, her voice heavy. "It would include their concerns, which would cast doubt on my integrity. If that happens, it'll be nearly impossible for me to publish again. It could ruin my career."

"Ruin your career?" Eric asked. "Is it really that serious?"

She nodded, her expression grim. "It is," she said. "Of course, there is a silver lining."

"What's that?" he asked.

"If my career is ruined, I won't have to worry about finding the money to keep the Center going," she said. "It'll die along with my reputation and career."

CHAPTER 38

Eric arrived at Carly's apartment ten minutes before the Zoom meeting was set to begin, carrying two steaming cups of coffee. His breath puffed out in small clouds, dissipating as quickly as they formed. The brisk March air clung to his jacket, and the aroma of roasted beans wafted through the chilly air as he knocked on her door.

Carly opened the door, her face a mix of tension and relief.

"I come bearing gifts," Eric said, handing her one of the cups.

"Bless you," she said, taking the cup and inhaling deeply as if it held the answer to all her worries. "I've been so focused on preparing for this meeting that I didn't even think about coffee." She took a long sip, her shoulders easing slightly. "It's perfect. Thank you."

Eric stepped inside, brushing the cold off his jacket as he took in the scene. Carly's apartment was always neat, but today it had an extra edge of precision, as if order could somehow tame the chaos she was bracing for. Her laptop was set up at the small dinette table, the soft blue glow of the video conferencing app waiting patiently on the screen. Papers were scattered in meticulous piles, a stark contrast to the storm swirling in Carly's mind.

"Are you ready?" He set his own cup down and slid into the chair opposite her.

Carly placed her coffee carefully on a coaster, her fingers lingering on the edge of the cup like it was her anchor. "I am, I think. But I'm nervous. There's so much riding on this. If they decide to pull the paper…" She trailed off, shaking her head slightly as though unwilling to give voice to her fears.

"Hey, you've got this." Eric leaned forward, his voice low and reassuring. "They'd be idiots not to see how solid your work is."

She smiled faintly, the corner of her lips twitching upward. "Thanks. Wish me luck anyway?"

"I don't think you'll need it, but good luck." He reached across the table and gave her hand a squeeze.

Carly exhaled deeply, her breath steadying as she straightened her posture. She clicked the link to join the meeting, and the screen sprang to life with a grid of faces. Each member of the review board appeared, their expressions neutral but sharp.

"Hello, Dr. Pellegrino," said a woman with an authoritative tone. Her hair was streaked with silver, and her glasses reflected the glow of her monitor. "Thank you for joining us this morning. Since this meeting is being recorded, I'd like to formally introduce everyone." She paused a moment and cleared her throat. "I am Dr. Cynthia Ellsworth, editor of the *Parapsychology Review.* Joining me today are Dr. Calvin Hubbard from the Yale University Department of Psychology, Dr. Rosemary Barnes from Stanford, and Dr. Ellis Monroe from the University of Michigan. Thank you all for convening on such short notice."

Each member of the board offered a brief acknowledgment. Carly nodded at each, her calm exterior hiding the racing thoughts Eric knew were running through her head.

"Dr. Pellegrino," Dr. Ellsworth continued, "we're here to address concerns regarding your recent paper. It has been brought to our attention that you are currently in a relationship with Mr. Eric Simms, the subject of your research, and that this was not disclosed during your submission process. Given the challenges and scrutiny our field often faces, it is imperative that we maintain the highest ethical standards. At this time, we would like to hear your explanation for this omission."

Carly folded her hands in front of her, her posture straight and composed, although Eric noticed the faintest tremor in her fingers.

"Eric Simms was referred to me by Dr. James Ferris, MD, a neurologist at Indianapolis Methodist Hospital and a professor at the Indiana University School of Medicine. Mr. Simms suffered head trauma as the result of an auto accident, and he was experiencing unexplained memories that he had not had prior to the accident."

Carly's voice was steady, and she gripped the edge of the table. She glanced briefly at the laptop camera, catching her own reflection in the small preview window. Her hair, carefully styled earlier, now had a stray curl falling rebelliously over her forehead. She tucked it back quickly, a fleeting sign of her nerves.

"It was an auto racing accident, was it not?" Dr. Hubbard asked, his tone clipped. His image on the screen, framed by the dark wooden bookcase behind him, gave him a stern, academic presence.

"That's right," Carly said, meeting his gaze through the screen. "The accident occurred while Mr. Simms was attempting to qualify for the Indianapolis 500."

"So, Mr. Simms is a professional race car driver?"

"That's right." Carly clasped her hands in her lap, out of view of the camera, her thumbs gently circling each other. "I interviewed Mr. Simms in my office and over the phone, recording our interviews with his approval. Following the interviews, I researched the information he provided concerning the memories he had of the life I wrote about in my paper, as well as other lives he was remembering."

Dr. Hubbard leaned forward slightly, his glasses catching the light. "There are other lives as well as the life you wrote about?"

Carly nodded. "There are," she said, her voice calm but deliberate. "However, the documentation I was able to uncover for those other lives was not as robust as the evidence I was able to find for the life I wrote about in the paper."

Dr. Barnes, her image softer and more inviting on the screen, tilted her head thoughtfully. "This is fine information," she said. "But what I'd like to know is why you didn't include a caveat in the paper about your personal relationship with Mr. Simms."

Carly took a measured breath. "Yes, of course," Her voice was steady and professional, tinged with a slight edge of vulnerability. "During the time I was conducting interviews with Mr. Simms, whilst I was conducting my research, during the period I was writing the paper, and even when I submitted the paper and it was accepted for publication, I did not have a relationship with Mr. Simms. It wasn't until after the paper was submitted for publication that we began seeing each other outside of our professional relationship."

Dr. Hubbard raised an eyebrow. "Are you saying you weren't dating Mr. Simms prior to your paper being accepted for publication?"

"That's right," Carly said, her gaze unwavering. "Had we been dating earlier, I would have included that information in the paper. In fact, I don't think I would have submitted the paper at all had we started dating earlier."

A faint smile played at the edges of Dr. Barnes' lips. "I don't think we can expect Dr. Pellegrino to notify us about a personal relationship before it occurs," she said, her tone laced with dry humor. "To the best of my knowledge, she's not clairvoyant."

Dr. Monroe's voice cut in, cooler and more clinical. "Perhaps not, but once the relationship began, wouldn't it have been prudent to inform the journal?"

"Even after the paper is published?" Dr. Barnes countered. "How long after publication does an author owe us that type of obligation?"

Dr. Ellsworth raised a hand, her silver-streaked hair catching the light as she did. "I think we should probably limit our discussion for now," she said. "We'll have a chance to discuss the situation once we end the Zoom call." Turning her attention back to Carly, her expression softened slightly. "Dr. Pellegrino, do you have anything you'd like to add?"

Carly met the gaze of the camera and paused a beat before answering. "I believe I've addressed the core concerns," she said, her voice even. "Thank you for giving me the opportunity to explain."

"Thank you, Dr. Pellegrino," Dr. Ellsworth said. "We'll notify you of our decision once our review is complete."

As the meeting ended, Carly let out a long breath, her body sagging against the chair as if the tension had physically drained her. "That was rubbish," she said, her voice tinged with exhaustion.

Eric leaned forward, a look of disbelief on his face. "Are you kidding? You were amazing. You made them look like amateurs."

She managed a weak smile, her eyes searching his for reassurance. "You think so?"

"I'd bet on you," Eric said, his tone unwavering. "You made a solid case."

Carly forced a weak smile. "Thanks, I hope you're right."

"So, what do you think will happen?"

"I think they're going to withdraw the article, attack me as a fraud, and ruin my career."

"That's the spirit," he said.

Carly laughed. "Maybe it won't be that bad. I'm just preparing myself for the worst."

"While you were on the call, I wanted to jump in and defend you," he said. "I would have told them that you submitted the article before I ever saw you naked or we had sex. We hadn't even had a date by that time."

"You make it sound like we didn't have a date before we had sex."

"We didn't," he said.

"Yes, we did," she said, her voice defiant. "We went out to dinner before we hopped into the sack." Carly used air quotes when she said, "hopped into the sack."

"That wasn't a date," Eric chided. "It was a business meeting."

"No, it wasn't. It was a date," Carly said. "You already knew I was Rachel."

"Sure, try explaining that to the editors."

They both laughed, and as they did, Carly's phone buzzed on the table, bringing an end to their brief happy moment. She glanced at the screen, lines appearing on her forehead. "It's Marlene, the editor who signed me to write the book." She answered the phone and put the call on speaker.

"Hello, Marlene. How are you?"

"How am I?" Marlene's thick New York accent crackled through the speaker, its sharpness cutting through the room. "I'm not the one with a bunch of religious zealots protesting outside my office. How are you holding up?"

Carly chuckled, the sound hollow. "Let's just say it's been a week."

"I'll bet," Marlene said dryly. "Listen, I'm calling about your book. As much as I'd love to poke the zealots, my bosses are nervous. They're not sure this book is worth the backlash."

Carly's grip on her coffee tightened. "Are you saying you're pulling the contract?"

Marlene hesitated, her silence heavy. "Not yet. But unless there's more to the story—something big and sensational—I can't guarantee we'll move forward. When we talked before, you told me about other lives that your guy lived. Is there an angle to the story that might attract more readers and sell more books?"

"I've documented five past lives, but the farther back in time we go, the less documentation there is."

"I'm not talking about documentation, sweety" Marlene said. "I'm talking about something more sensational. Something sexy or super controversial. Like maybe Eric was Cleopatra's lover in a previous life. Or hell, maybe he *was* Cleopatra."

"No, nothing like that," Carly explained. "That's not the kind…"

Before Carly could respond fully, Eric leaned forward, his voice cutting through the air. "Marlene, this is Eric. I have something sensational for you. Carly doesn't even know about it yet. Can you give us a couple of weeks to work out the details? I promise, you won't be sorry"

Carly's eyes widened in shock, her lips forming a silent question: *What the hell are you doing?*

"The boyfriend comes to the rescue," Marlene said with a laugh. "I like it. Very romantic. I can give you some time, but whatever you're doing, it had better be good."

Eric grinned, his eyes alight with determination. "Trust me, Marlene. You're going to love it."

CHAPTER 39

Carly shot up from her chair, her eyes wide with disbelief. "Are you crazy?" Her voice was tinged with equal parts alarm and frustration. "This is legitimate research. You can't just make things up because a book publisher wants a sensational story to help her sell books."

Eric raised his hands defensively, the gesture almost pleading. "I'm not making up anything." His voice was soft, his tone measured, as if trying to defuse the storm brewing in Carly's eyes. "There's something I haven't been telling you, Carly. Something I've been too embarrassed to say out loud. Too afraid of what you might think. But you deserve to know."

Carly tilted her head, her eyes wide. "Did you cheat on me when I was Rachel?"

Eric's shoulders relaxed, and he let out an involuntary laugh. "What? No. Why would you even think that?"

She shrugged, her eyes darting away momentarily. "I guess I have trust issues."

"No, it's not that." Shaking his head, Eric leaned forward, his hands gripping the table, as if the weight of what he had to tell her needed the support of something solid. "It's much bigger than cheating on you."

Carly sank back into her chair, exhaling slowly. Her hands rested on her lap, her fingers fidgeting with the hem of her sweater. "Whatever it is, it won't matter if you can't prove it." Her voice had calmed, but her resolve remained insistent. "No matter how great the story is, if we can't confirm that it actually happened, people will just roll their eyes. They won't care. And it will do more harm to my research than it will help. Do you understand?"

Eric smiled faintly. "I understand, but I need you to understand. You shouldn't worry. I can prove it."

Her eyes narrowed slightly, curiosity beginning to outpace her subsiding irritation. "Okay, then. What is it?"

Eric stood abruptly, pacing a few steps toward the window before turning back to her. "Let's sit in the living room." He motioned for her to follow him.

Carly hesitated, studying him for a moment before pushing herself up from her chair. She followed him into the living room, her footsteps soft against the hardwood floor. They both settled onto the couch. Eric leaned forward as if bracing himself for the weight of his confession.

He opened his mouth to speak, but the words seemed to catch in his throat. After a moment, he stood again, as if propelled by restless energy. "I'm going to open a bottle of wine," he said, already halfway to the kitchen.

Carly raised an eyebrow, her arms crossing in front of her. "It's ten o'clock in the morning," she called after him. "I thought you didn't drink before noon."

Eric turned back briefly, a hint of a smile playing on his lips. "Trust me. We'll need this."

Eric returned with two glasses of wine, setting them carefully on the coffee table before sinking heavily onto the couch. He picked up his glass and took a big gulp, his stiff movements revealing his tension.

Carly stared at him, her glass untouched. "Whatever this is, it must be pretty big," she said. "I've never seen you guzzle wine before."

"You might want to do the same," he said.

Carly lifted her glass hesitantly, taking a measured sip. She waited, holding the glass in both hands, her eyes fixed on Eric.

He took another long drink, then set his glass down with a soft clink. "Before I tell you the story, just remember—it wasn't me who did what I'm about to say. It was Ted Humphrey."

Carly tilted her head, her brows knitting together in confusion. "Ted?"

Eric nodded. "Yeah. I just don't want you to think badly of me for something he did. I know I used to be him, but I'm not anymore. I would never do what he did."

Carly's lips parted slightly as she absorbed his words. She nodded slowly, her expression softening but still cautious. "I understand. It wasn't you. It was Ted."

Eric exhaled deeply, steeling himself for what he was about to say. He cleared his throat, his gaze darting briefly to the wineglass before returning to Carly. "When John Driggins told me—I mean, told Ted—that he knew I'd slept with his wife and that he was taking all our money to Arizona, I panicked. I had a gun in my desk drawer, and I—" The words weighed heavily on his tongue. "I shot him. I killed him, Carly."

The story had come out much more quickly than he anticipated. He just blurted it out, and now the air between them seemed to freeze, the gravity of his confession hanging heavy in the room. Carly's eyes widened, her mouth opening slightly as if to speak, but no words came.

"Without John's money, the company was broke," he said. "And without the company, I was broke. I killed him so he couldn't move to Arizona, so he couldn't take the money."

Carly blinked, her grip on the wineglass tightening. "You killed him?" She spoke slowly, her voice barely above a whisper.

Eric nodded slowly, his shoulders slumping as if the admission had physically drained him.

"And you never got caught?"

"You mean Ted," he said. "No, he never got caught."

"What happened to the body?" Carly's voice was steadier now, but her fingers trembled slightly as she brought the glass closer to her chest, clutching it like a shield.

Eric leaned back against the couch, his gaze fixed on the blank TV screen, unable to meet her gaze. "I loaded John's body into the trunk of his car, then I started driving. I knew I had to get rid of the body, but I wasn't sure where to dump it. I thought about my uncle's lake cabin in Wisconsin. I'd seen my Uncle Emil earlier that day in Chicago, so I knew the cabin was empty. Even though it was a five- or six-hour drive up to the cabin, it made sense. It was far out of the way, and no one would ever think to look up there. So, I drove John's body to Rhinelander and buried him on my uncle's property."

"And he's still there?" Carly asked.

"As far as I know."

Carly put a hand to her mouth, her fingers pressing against her lips as if to hold back a gasp. "Oh my God."

Eric turned to her, his eyes searching hers. "Do you think less of me because of what I did?"

"No," she said quickly. She set her glass down on the coffee table and reached for his hand. "Like you said, that wasn't you. You were a different person in a much different situation, living in a different time."

He nodded, then kissed her hand. They sat in silence as the weight of Eric's confession settled over them.

"What do we do now?" Carly asked.

Eric reached for his wineglass, draining the last of its contents before setting it back on the table. He turned to Carly and exhaled forcefully. "I think we should go to Wisconsin and dig up John Driggins' body."

Chapter 40

They parked in the lot at the back of the building, the sound of the engine fading into the crisp Chicago morning. Eric turned off the ignition but remained still, gripping the steering wheel as if bracing for impact. The Chicago Police Department loomed ahead of them, its facade a blend of utilitarian brickwork and imposing authority. For a moment, the car's silence amplified the distant cacophony of city life—sirens wailing faintly in the distance, the honking of horns.

"Are you okay?" Carly asked.

Eric nodded, but his jaw tightened. "Just… thinking."

"About what?" Carly's hand reached across the console, resting lightly on his arm.

He sighed, his gaze fixed on the unassuming glass doors of the station. "Do you think they'll arrest me?" He hated to bring up the subject, but the closer they got to telling the police what they knew, the more he worried about his freedom.

Carly's eyes widened. "No, of course not, Eric. They can't arrest you for something that happened before you were born. It's impossible."

"But they don't know what we know," he said. "What if they decide the murder happened more recently? What if they think I'm some lunatic trying to cover my tracks by leading them to a body?"

Carly frowned, shifting in her seat to face him fully. "If you're worried about getting arrested, why are we even doing this?"

"For the book," he said. "You need that publishing contract. You've worked too hard for this, Carly. If we don't do it, we'll always wonder what could've been."

Her eyes softened, and she leaned closer. "That might be the sweetest thing anyone has ever done for me, love. But the contract isn't worth you being arrested. If I thought for a second that they would or could arrest you, I wouldn't let you do this. But I just don't see any way that can happen."

Eric nodded. Carly's words of encouragement didn't alleviate all his concerns, but they helped. "Okay then, let's do this."

They exited the car and made their way across the parking lot. The wind carried a sharp chill, cutting through their jackets as they approached the entrance. Inside, the station buzzed with activity. Uniformed officers and civilians migrated through the space, their voices blending into a low murmur. Fluorescent lights cast a cold, industrial glow over the linoleum floors and scarred beige walls, adding to the stark atmosphere.

At the front desk, a uniformed officer looked up from his computer. "Can I help you?"

"We're here to see Detective Nick Brunson," Eric said. "He's expecting us."

The officer picked up the phone, spoke briefly, then gestured toward a set of chairs along the wall. "He'll be out in a minute. You can wait there."

Eric and Carly sat side by side in the stiff plastic chairs. The room smelled faintly of coffee and cleaning solution. Eric's leg bounced with nervous energy, his fingers drumming lightly against his thigh.

Carly sighed. "He's not going to believe our story, is he?"

Eric's lips twitching into a slight smile. "We'll have to make him believe us."

The minutes dragged by until a thickly built man approached. Detective Nick Brunson had a square jaw and close-cropped hair, his short-sleeved shirt exposing muscular forearms despite the cool early

April air. His expression was unreadable, his dark eyes assessing them as he stopped a few feet away.

"I'm Detective Nick Brunson," he said, his voice low and gravelly. "Come with me." Without waiting for a response, he turned and walked away from them.

Eric and Carly exchanged a glance before following, winding their way down narrow hallways and through several rooms with cluttered desks. The police officers they encountered didn't pay any attention to them.

Brunson led them into a small, windowless office, gesturing to two scarred wooden chairs on one side of his desk. He took the seat on the other, his broad frame filling the space. Behind him, commendations in black plastic frames adorned the cement block wall. A blue sport coat hung on a hook in the corner, and a single photo of a younger Brunson with a woman and two kids sat on the desk beside a stack of manila folders.

"When you called, you said you had information about a missing persons case from 1984," Brunson said, picking up a thin folder. "A guy named John Driggins. We don't have much on him, just a report and a couple of tips that went nowhere. So, what can you tell me?"

Eric leaned forward, his palms resting on his knees. "He didn't go missing," he said. "I killed him. In 1984."

Brunson raised an eyebrow, his lips curling into a skeptical smirk. "Right. What year were you born?"

A wry smile spread across Eric's face. "I was born in 1995."

Brunson's eyes narrowed as he did the math. "So, you're 29 years old now and claim to have murdered a man who went missing eleven years before you were born."

Eric glanced at Carly, who gave him a reassuring nod. He took a deep breath. "Before we go further, you should probably know who we are." Eric explained that he was a professional race car driver and Carly was a psychologist doing research into past lives. He explained about the accident and how he started having memories of other people's lives.

"And for our purposes today, in 1984, I was a guy named Ted Humphrey," Eric said.

Brunson's expression remained impassive, though his pencil tapped a slow rhythm against the desk.

Eric took a deep breath, then continued. "In 1984, Ted was in business with John Driggins. They owned a construction company. Driggins found out Ted was sleeping with his wife and confronted him. He said he was pulling his money out of the business and was moving to Arizona. Without his money, the business was finished. Ted panicked, grabbed a gun, and shot him."

Brunson leaned back, his chair creaking. "Bravo," he said, slow clapping. "That's quite a story, especially with the reincarnation angle. What's next? A reality show pitch?"

Carly exhaled audibly, slumping slightly in her chair. Eric smiled faintly, undeterred. "There's more," he said. "I know where Driggins' body is buried. I can take you to it."

Brunson's smirk faded. "You know where he's buried?"

Eric nodded. "After Ted shot him, he wrapped the body in Visqueen…"

"In what?"

"Visqueen. You know, sheets of plastic. We used to use it as a vapor barrier when building new homes," Eric said. "Anyway, I went down the street where we were building another home and brought it back to the model where I'd shot Driggins. I wrapped him in it and carried him to his car, which was parked in front of the model home. I put him in the trunk, then drove the car to my uncle's cabin up in Rhinelander. I buried him and the gun up there, then took his car to a local salvage yard and had it crushed. For $500, they didn't ask any questions."

Brunson tapped his pencil more deliberately now, the rhythm slower but heavier. "Rhinelander," he repeated thoughtfully. "And you're saying you can lead us to the exact spot?"

"That's right."

The detective turned his attention to Carly. "Do you go along with all this, Doc?"

Carly sat up straighter in her chair. "I do. I've corroborated Eric's memories with documentation. I even spoke with Driggins' ex-wife, who confirmed the affair."

Brunson stared at her for a long moment, his pencil now still. Finally, he sighed. "Even if I believed you—and I'm not saying I do—if we go up to Rhinelander and there's no body, I'm the idiot who fell for a ghost story. I don't like looking like an idiot. Do you understand?"

Carly leaned forward, placing her hands on the edge of Brunson's metal desk. "Detective, I don't blame you for not believing us. It's a sensational story that sounds like it's made up by a couple of mental patients."

Eric turned and looked at Carly. "Hon, I don't think that's helpful."

Carly put up her hand, quieting Eric. "But I've looked into all of Eric's other claims. They all check out. There were a few things from long ago previous lives that I couldn't confirm, meaning I couldn't find documentation to support his memories. But there was nothing that Eric shared with me from his memories that was wrong. There's nothing I've been able to find to contradict or disprove what he's told me. He's telling you the truth, and all you have to do to confirm what we've just told you and to solve a decades-old murder is to drive to Rhinelander and dig a hole."

Brunson sat back in his chair and exhaled. "I don't believe in reincarnation."

"What we believe or don't believe doesn't change the truth," Carly said. "I can't prove to you that reincarnation is real. What I can tell you is that I have investigated numerous cases, including Eric's, and I can't come up with a more plausible explanation. What you believe or don't believe doesn't change the fact that the body of John Driggins, killed in 1984 in Chicago, is buried up in Rhinelander, Wisconsin. And now that you know where it is, I suspect you're going to want to go up there and retrieve it."

Brunson was quiet for a moment, then opened the thin manila folder and began reading aloud. "John Driggins co-owned DH Homes with Theodore Humphrey. Shortly after Driggins disappeared, Humphrey sold his house in Lincolnwood and moved to Rhinelander, where he died in 1991."

Eric nodded. "You've done some research."

Brunson closed the folder with a sigh. "It'll take a while to set this up. I'll call you when we're ready."

CHAPTER 41

As they stepped out of the police station, the chill of the April breeze wrapped around them, winter's icy grip not yet ready to let loose. The midday sun fought to break through the clouds, casting faint streaks of light on the concrete sidewalk. Carly shivered and instinctively reached for Eric's hand, lacing her fingers through his.

"How do you think it went?" she asked.

Eric gave her hand a squeeze, the warmth of her touch a welcome source of reassurance. "Pretty good, I'd say. I didn't get arrested, and it looks like we're going to Rhinelander." He stopped abruptly, turning to face her. Placing his hands gently on her shoulders, he looked into her eyes, the corners of his mouth lifting into a small, appreciative smile. "You were fantastic in there. I don't think Brunson believed me, but he trusted you."

Carly stepped back with a flourish, placing a hand over her stomach as she gave an exaggerated bow. "Thank you very much," she said, her tone playful.

The gesture pulled a laugh from Eric, and he reached for her hand as they walked to the parking lot.

At the car, Eric slid into the driver's seat but didn't immediately start the engine. Instead, he stared at the steering wheel, his hands resting on the cool leather, tracing its stitched grooves.

Carly tilted her head, studying him. "What are you thinking?"

He hesitated, wrestling with whether to speak the thoughts that had been circling his mind since revealing his secret. Finally, he turned to her. "Are you sure none of this bothers you?"

"What do you mean?" Carly asked, shifting in her seat to face him.

"You know," he said. "The fact that your boyfriend is a murderer."

Carly's expression softened into a mixture of amusement and exasperation. "My boyfriend isn't a murderer," she said firmly. "My boyfriend is Eric Simms. Ted Humphrey was a murderer." Reaching across the console, she placed her hand over his. "You're not Ted."

Eric let out a short laugh, shaking his head. "You know what I mean. That was me, or at least another version of me."

Carly's gaze didn't waver. "You experienced Ted's life, yes. But you're not Ted any more than I'm Rachel. We've lived different lives, made different choices. You can't hold yourself responsible for something you didn't do."

He studied her face, searching for any hint of doubt. Her conviction was unshakable, but his own wasn't as firm. "If they end up arresting me, I want you on my jury."

Carly laughed, the sound relieving some of the tension he felt. "I don't see how they can arrest you. You haven't done anything wrong."

Eric nodded, though her assurance wasn't enough to completely silence his fears. "I've been thinking about this," he said. "I'm hoping they can somehow date when the murder took place. But what if they can't? What if they think Driggins was killed recently? I mean, I'm the one who told them about it. I'm the one who knows where the body is buried."

Carly chuckled. "And you concocted this elaborate scheme to get into a big, very public racing accident, suffer major head trauma, and claim you're having memories of past lives—all to cover up murdering Driggins—a man you couldn't have possibly known—years after he went missing? That's quite a plan."

Eric laughed despite himself, the absurdity of her words breaking through his unease. "Yeah, I guess it is kind of farfetched."

Leaning over, he kissed her briefly, a gesture of gratitude as much as affection. Then, with a deep breath, he started the car. They drove in silence, the cityscape gradually giving way to quieter streets. Eric's thoughts drifted, pulling him back into the tangled web of memories that weren't quite his but felt as vivid as any of his own.

He thought of Ted Humphrey—the man whose life now haunted his dreams. Ted had been a heavy-drinking, selfish, morally bankrupt man who had slept with his business partner's wife and killed him in a desperate attempt to keep his crumbling business afloat. The memory of pulling the trigger was seared into Eric's mind, as real and visceral as if he had done it himself.

How had he ever been that person? How could the man he was now—a man who cared deeply for Carly, who couldn't fathom harming anyone—have once been so ruthless? Carly had called the memories a blessing, but they often felt like a curse. Still, he couldn't deny that they had led him to her. For that, he supposed, he could be grateful.

Carly's phone rang, jolting him from his half-conscious stupor. She glanced at the screen and her eyebrows lifted. "It's Dr. Ellsworth from Parapsychology Review," she said, her voice tight.

Eric raised his eyebrows in return. "Good luck," he said, his tone laced with encouragement and curiosity.

She answered, her voice composed but cautious. "Hello, Dr. Ellsworth." The conversation was brief, punctuated by Carly saying, "I understand," and "Thank you for letting me know" several times. When she hung up, her shoulders slumped slightly.

"You didn't say much," Eric noted, glancing at her.

"Dr. Ellsworth did most of the talking," she said. "She wanted to let me know what they decided about my paper."

"And?" Eric prompted.

"They're not pulling it," Carly said. "But they're adding a statement clarifying that the author became involved in a personal relationship with the subject after the research was conducted."

Eric considered this, then nodded. "That's not so bad, is it?"

"I suppose not," she admitted, though her tone carried a trace of irritation. "It's better than having the article pulled, but it irks me that the journal is so quick to cover their tracks. They published the article because they thought it was worthwhile. They should stand behind it instead of bending over backwards to appease potential critics."

Eric reached for her hand. "After we visit Rhinelander and you write your book, it won't matter what they think."

She looked at him, her lips curving into a faint smile. "I hope you're right."

CHAPTER 42

The northern Wisconsin sky was a brilliant expanse of blue, unbroken except for the occasional whisper of a passing cloud. The sun hung high, its pale light bouncing off the bare branches of trees, but it offered no respite from the biting chill that clung to the air. Although the ground was clear of snow, a brittle frost coated the edges of fallen leaves and the dormant grass. The rhythmic chugging of the backhoe echoed through the quiet woods, filling the morning with a mechanical hum that drowned out most other sounds. Eric and Carly stood side by side, silent as they watched the machine's massive bucket tear into the frozen earth, each scoop sending a shiver through the ground beneath their feet.

Through the skeletal trees, Eric caught glimpses of Velvet Lake, its surface shimmering like liquid mercury under the pale sunlight. It felt strange to stand here again, not as himself, but as someone who had once been Ted Humphrey. Ted had fished in these waters many times, knew the hidden pockets where bass and walleye lingered, and had drowned here in an act of careless drunkenness. Eric's memories of this place were vivid yet disjointed, a mosaic of sensations and emotions from a life that wasn't entirely his own. The familiar paths leading to the lake, the isolated serenity of the cabin, and the hollow thud of the backhoe's bucket hitting soil—it was all too real.

It had taken Detective Brunson just over two weeks to arrange the dig with his counterparts in Rhinelander. During that time, Eric had ventured out to California and raced in the Grand Prix of Long Beach. The weekend had been a success. He finished second, close behind the race winner, Alexander Rossi. The team was ecstatic. It was their first podium finish, and Eric was proud to have been the one to accomplish it for them. They celebrated late into the night, the whole team confident a race victory was in their future.

Now, in the chilly Wisconsin sunshine, that moment in Long Beach felt like it had happened long ago and a million miles away. Eric glanced at Carly, her breath visible in the crisp air, and wondered if she sensed his unease. She hadn't said much since they arrived. But her hand occasionally brushed against his arm, a silent reassurance he appreciated more than words, and a sure sign that she knew, at least on an empathic level, what he was feeling.

Detective Brunson approached the area where Eric and Carly stood, his sturdy frame casting a shadow over them. He was joined by a local police officer, a tall, wiry man with a weathered face and a distinct Wisconsin accent. "This is Detective Myers from the Oneida County Sheriff's Office." Brunson gestured toward his companion. "He's in charge of this dig."

Myers nodded curtly at Eric, his breath fogging the air. "So, you're the one who knew where the body was buried," he said, his voice raised to compete with the backhoe's rumble.

Eric met Myers' gaze and spoke loudly. "I buried it here in a previous life," he said. "Not in this one. It wasn't me who killed him, not really. It was Ted Humphrey. I'm not him anymore."

Myers blinked, his brow furrowing deeply. "You what now?"

Brunson intervened, placing a hand on Myers' arm. "I'll explain later," he said. "For now, just know that if we don't find a body here, you can help me bury Mr. Simms in that hole."

Myers opened his mouth, then closed it again, apparently unable to respond. He shook his head.

"Let's see how the digging's going." Brunson motioned Myers back toward the excavation site.

"That went well," Carly said, watching the two detectives' retreat.

Eric chuckled. "Yeah, I really think we're winning them over."

As the backhoe paused to adjust its angle, Eric noticed a man and a woman standing off to the side. The man wore a brown Carhartt jacket stretched tight over a round belly, a steaming cup of coffee cradled in his gloved hands. Something about him tugged at Eric's memory, a faint sense of familiarity that felt both foreign and unsettling. When their eyes met, the man leaned toward the woman, saying something that Eric couldn't hear over the sound of the backhoe, then the pair walked toward Eric and Carly.

The man extended his hand as he approached. "I'm Phil Humphrey," he said. His grip firm, his smile earnest. "This is my wife, Amanda. We own this place."

Eric shook his hand, the name sparking recognition that sent a buzz up his spine. "Nice to meet you." He introduced Carly, and as he did, his thoughts raced. Phil Humphrey. His cousin. In another life.

"I'm an IndyCar fan," Phil said. "I've been following your story about all this reincarnation stuff. So, you used to be Ted Humphrey?"

Eric hesitated, glancing briefly at Carly before nodding. "I think so."

Phil's smile widened. "Can you tell me about him? About Ted?"

"You want to know about Ted?" Eric asked, caught off guard by the request.

Phil nodded earnestly. "You were my cousin, and my dad always said if it wasn't for you, we wouldn't have been able to keep the cabin in the family. I was just a kid when you were alive, so I don't remember you all that well."

Eric hesitated, unsure of how much to reveal. His memories of Ted weren't flattering—selfishness, alcoholism, and ultimately, murder. "I'm afraid I—or Ted—wasn't a very good person," he said carefully. "I drank too much, I was selfish, and I killed the man buried over there." He gestured toward the excavation site, his voice dropping slightly. "I don't think I was anyone you'd have wanted to know."

Phil frowned, shaking his head. "That doesn't sound like the Ted my dad talked about. He always said Ted rented the cabin out so my dad could pay the mortgage after he lost his job. And when the place needed repairs, Ted did the work himself and paid for the materials out of his own pocket. He even helped pay for my mom's funeral."

"She had an aneurysm," Eric said softly, the words slipping out before he realized he'd spoken.

Phil's eyes widened. "You remember?"

Eric hesitated, then nodded slowly. "I guess I do."

"For what it's worth," Phil continued, his tone growing more reflective, "Ted was held in high regard in our family. We admired him. I don't know what all this is about"—he gestured toward the backhoe, its bucket clawing at the earth—"but it doesn't sound like something Ted would've done. And if he did, he must've had a good reason."

Eric stared at him, the weight of Phil's words sinking in. "You admired Ted," his words as much a question as a statement.

"We did. My dad thought the world of him. He was devastated when you died so young, especially since you died here at our place." Phil motioned toward the cabin behind him.

A strange warmth bloomed in Eric's chest, tempered by guilt. "Really?" he said quietly. "I didn't think anyone would've missed me."

"Oh, yeah," Phil said, his voice firm. "Because of what you did for the family when my mom died, my dad helped pay for your funeral."

"That's… nice," Eric said, his throat tight. "Thanks for sharing that with me."

Phil reached into his back pocket and pulled out a thick brown leather wallet. Flipping it open, he retrieved a worn photograph and held it out to Eric. "This is a picture of Ted with my dad, me, and my brother. Donnie and I were just little kids. That's Ted on the left."

Eric stared at the photo, his breath catching. The man in the picture—Ted—looked eerily like him. The same mop of brown hair. The same angular facial features. Ted even stood the same way as Eric, his hands self-consciously tucked in his front pants packets. "Oh my gosh," he murmured, his voice barely audible.

Carly leaned in to look. "Can I see that?"

Phil handed her the photo, and she studied it closely before looking up at Eric. "That's incredible. He looks just like you."

Phil glanced between the photo and Eric, his brow furrowing. "My gosh, she's right. The two of you could be twins."

Eric rubbed his chin, the revelation unsettling. "How can that be?" he asked. "We're not related. We come from completely different families."

"There's some research suggesting that from one life to the next, people often look similar," Carly said. "It's not a theory I've subscribed to, but this is hard to ignore."

Phil slid the photo back into his wallet and returned it to his pocket. "Well, it was nice meeting you," he said. "I'll be cheering for you this year."

Eric shook his hand again, murmuring a quiet thanks as Phil and Amanda walked back toward the cabin—the same cabin Eric had once called home in another lifetime.

"Are you okay?" Carly asked, her voice gentle.

Eric nodded slowly, though his thoughts were a swirling storm. "Yeah, I was just surprised to hear about a side of Ted I don't remember. And that photo, wow."

The sound of the backhoe suddenly stopped, breaking through their conversation. A police officer's voice rang out over the still air. "We got something."

CHAPTER 43

The backhoe's engine sputtered to a halt, leaving an eerie silence in its wake. The sound of the machine had become a kind of shield, a distraction that muffled the gravity of what was happening. Without it, the weight of the moment bore down on Eric. The chill in the northern Wisconsin air seemed sharper now, biting through his jacket and chilling him to his core. Nearby, the Rhinelander police detectives gathered around the freshly dug hole, their breath visible in the cold air as they spoke and examined the unearthed ground.

One of the detectives leaned into the hole, pulling up a corner of muddied plastic sheeting. He straightened, holding the torn fragment at arm's length. "Is this anything?"

Detective Myers stepped forward, his boots crunching against the frost-covered ground. "It could be," he said, his tone neutral. "We'd better start digging by hand."

The backhoe operator maneuvered the machine away from the hole, its hulking frame retreating like a giant animal slinking into the trees. Two Rhinelander officers grabbed shovels from the bed of a nearby truck and moved in, their movements deliberate as they carefully dug into the cold, packed earth. Each scoop of soil revealed a little more of the secrets hidden below.

Minutes passed before an officer's shovel struck something solid. He crouched, brushing soil away with gloved hands. "I've got something." He held up what appeared to be a man's shoe. Dirt caked its surface, but the shape was unmistakable. He dropped it into a plastic evidence bag and handed it to Detective Myers.

"Better change to hand trowels," Myers said. "Dig carefully. Look for any small bits of evidence. I don't want to miss anything."

The officers exchanged their shovels for smaller tools, kneeling by the edge of the hole as they scraped away the soil with meticulous precision.

"Hold on," Brunson said, glancing over his shoulder. "Eric, come over here."

Eric froze. His stomach twisted into a tight knot. He had been standing a safe distance away with Carly, intentionally avoiding the scene. The idea of seeing what remained of John Driggins—of facing the consequences of what Ted had done—filled him with a dread he hadn't anticipated. But Brunson's expectant look left no room for hesitation.

Eric approached the edge of the hole reluctantly, his feet feeling heavier with each step. When he reached Brunson, he glanced down and felt an immediate wave of relief. For now, all he could see was dirt and a sliver of the plastic sheeting.

"Do you remember how you buried the body?" Brunson asked, his voice low and direct. "What direction was the grave running?"

Eric swallowed hard, forcing himself to dig into the murky depths of Ted's memories. He had spent so much energy trying to suppress them, pushing away the images and feelings tied to that night. Now, Brunson was asking him to retrieve those memories, to relive them. He closed his eyes briefly, the chill air stinging his face as he focused.

"I think…," he hesitated. "I think it was parallel to the shoreline," he said finally, pointing to his left. "The grave would go out that way."

Brunson nodded, gesturing for the officers to continue digging in that direction. Eric took a step back, eager to retreat to Carly's side.

When he reached her, Carly slipped her arm through his, her touch warm and reassuring. "You look pale," she said, her eyes searching his face. "Are you okay?"

Eric rubbed his face with one hand, the other gripping Carly's arm for support. "I didn't think it would hit me this hard."

"You didn't do this," Carly reminded him gently. Her voice was soothing, steady. "Ted did. You're not him anymore."

He nodded, wanting to believe her. Logically, he knew she was right—he wasn't Ted. But the guilt bore down on him like a shadow he couldn't shake. The memory didn't just belong to Ted, it was his now, vivid and visceral.

The memories came flooding back, unbidden and unwelcome. The ground had been softer that night, making the digging easier, but the task still took hours. He could still feel the weight of the shovel in his hands, the strain in his muscles as he dug that grave. Every movement was laced with panic and dread. He remembered tossing the gun into the hole before dragging Driggins' lifeless body from the car. Driggins had been heavy—heavier than Ted had anticipated. He recalled the moment when one of Driggins' shoes slipped off as he stumbled toward the grave, though he hadn't noticed it at the time. It was only later, as he was covering the body with dirt, that he spotted the shoe lying in the grass. He had thrown it into the grave without a second thought and continued shoveling until there was no trace of what lay beneath.

"Eric?" Carly's voice cut through his thoughts.

He blinked, looking at her. "What?"

"They found the body," she said, pointing toward the hole.

Eric turned, his stomach lurching as he saw the officers lifting a dark, soil-covered form from the ground. The remains of John Driggins.

"Oh, God…" Eric said.

Brunson, standing nearby, raised an eyebrow. "What's wrong with you? I thought you didn't kill him."

"I didn't," Eric said, his throat tight. "But I remember doing it."

"Right," Brunson said, his tone skeptical. "In a past life." He crossed his arms. "I've got to tell you, I'm not sure I buy this reincarnation angle. In my line of work, we deal with evidence, not theories."

Carly stepped forward to join the conversation. "In my line of work, too, Detective" she said, gesturing toward the unearthed body. "And that's evidence."

Eric glanced at Brunson. "You don't think I did it, do you?"

"You, or the mythical Ted?" Brunson asked.

"Me."

Brunson shook his head, brushing dirt off his hands. "No. That body has been there a long time. Decades, I would guess. I don't think you did it, Eric. But that doesn't mean I'm convinced about reincarnation."

"Like I told you before," Carly said, "what we believe doesn't change the facts."

Eric hesitated before speaking again. "There's one more thing," he said. "The murder weapon should be in the hole. It was under the body."

Brunson stared at him for a moment, his expression unreadable. "That's quite a memory you've got there." Without another word, he turned and strode toward the hole to relay Eric's information to the other police officers.

CHAPTER 44

Eric drove away from the cabin with a sense of quiet unease, the Wisconsin woods stretching endlessly in his rearview mirror. The cabin—once his home in another life—seemed to loom in his mind's eye long after it had disappeared from sight. It wasn't just the physical place, with its rustic wooden beams and the faint smell of pine and wood smoke that lingered in the air; it was the memories it stirred, memories that weren't technically his but that lived inside him nonetheless. The sharp edges of regret, shame, and guilt pricked at him, but there was a flicker of something softer too, something that Phil Humphrey had offered—a glimpse of redemption, of kindness woven into the fabric of Ted's otherwise frayed and flawed life.

Beside him, Carly sat silently, her gaze fixed on him rather than the passing scenery. Her presence in his life was a steading force. She had a way of pulling him back to the present when his thoughts threatened to spiral.

"What?" Eric finally asked, breaking the silence but keeping his eyes on the road.

"I'm just watching you," she said. "You're being a bit quiet."

"Am I?" He glanced at her briefly, a small, tired smile on his lips. "I guess being back at the cabin has my mind racing."

Carly tilted her head, studying him as if she could pull the full story from his expression alone. "Is that it?"

Eric frowned, unsure how to respond. "What do you mean?"

"Is that all you're going to say on the subject?"

He hesitated. He didn't want to talk about Ted anymore. The memories were starting to feel too real, too present, like they could somehow bleed into his current life if he dwelled on them too much. Instead, he decided to change the subject. "What do you think Marlene will have to say about all this? Do you think she'll be ready to move forward with the book?"

Carly gave him a knowing look but allowed the subject to change. "I think she'll be thrilled," she admitted. "She loves sensational, and all of this is pretty sensational."

"Why don't you call her and tell her?"

"Right now?"

"Why not?" Eric shrugged. "The sooner you get the book deal done, the sooner you'll have money for the Center."

Carly sighed, leaning back in her seat. "Truthfully, I don't think the book will help the Center much. This isn't like a Stephen King novel. My advance isn't huge, maybe enough to keep the Center going for a couple of weeks. If the book sells really well or I can sell the movie rights, which is doubtful, I might make a decent amount of money. But if any of that happens, it will take time. The Center needs money now."

Eric considered her words, his fingers drumming lightly against the steering wheel. He didn't know much about publishing, but Carly's pragmatism was sobering. "It still sounds like pinning Marlene down as soon as possible is the best course of action."

"You're probably right," Carly conceded, pulling out her phone. "I'll call her now."

"Put it on speaker," Eric said with a grin. "I want to hear."

Carly rolled her eyes but complied, dialing the number and waiting as the line connected. Marlene answered, her voice immediately cutting through with her characteristic sharpness. "Do you have something sensational to tell me?"

Carly couldn't help but laugh. "In fact, I do." She launched into the story, recounting the murder of John Driggins and the recovery of his body with a calmness that belied the enormity of what they'd just experienced.

"Holy shit," Marlene said, drawing out the syllables with dramatic flair. "I asked for sensational, and you really delivered."

"Does that mean you want to move forward with the contract?"

"Abso-friggin-lutely," Marlene said. "I want to see a first draft of the book as soon as you can get it to me."

"I'll start working on it right away," Carly promised. "Thanks, Marlene. I'll be in touch."

When the call ended, Eric chuckled, shaking his head. "She's pretty excited. Maybe you should renegotiate the advance."

"I wish," Carly said. "Unfortunately, I think it's too late for that."

Eric pulled into the motel parking lot, the car crunching over uneven pavement as he parked. They stepped out, the cold air nipping at their cheeks as they hurried inside.

"What do you think Kevin will say about this when he finds out?" Carly asked.

"I'm not sure," Eric admitted. "But I need to call him. He needs to hear this from me."

Inside the room, Carly flopped onto the bed, her back against the headboard, while Eric sank into an overstuffed chair. He pulled out his phone, dialed Kevin's number, and put the call on speaker so Carly could listen.

Eric kept his tone casual as he explained to Kevin that he had some news to share about his ongoing past life saga. Kevin suggested they loop in Dennis, and after a brief runaround with receptionists, the familiar Australian accent came on the line.

"Hello, Kevin," Dennis said. "To what do I owe the pleasure?"

"Hello, Dennis," Kevin said. "I have Eric on the line with us, and he just told me he has some big news to share about his past life drama. Rather than have him tell the story twice, I thought we'd get you on the line so we can hear it at the same time."

"Good thinking," Dennis said. "How are you, Eric? Have you recovered from that brilliant drive in Long Beach? Your podium finish was impressive."

"I have," Eric said. "And I'm looking forward to doing even better at Barber."

"I hope so," Dennis said. "So, what is this story you have to tell us?"

Eric hesitated, his mouth suddenly dry. He realized this wasn't just a story, it was a gamble, one that could cost him his career. He cleared his throat. "Let me start by saying how much I appreciate driving for you and how I hope what I'm about to tell you doesn't change that."

"Oh, oh," Kevin said. "This can't be good."

"Maybe it's best for you to just tell us the story," Dennis said.

Eric took a deep breath, then exhaled slowly. "You both know that I have memories of being Ted Humphrey. Back in the 1970s, I—well, Ted—was a partner in a home construction business with a guy named John Driggins. Ted had the building knowledge, and John had the money. Anyway, John found out that Ted was sleeping with his wife. Naturally, John was angry and told Ted he was pulling his money out of the business and moving to Arizona."

Eric hesitated, but knew he had to continue. There was no going back. He glanced at Carly, who was sitting on the bed with her back to the wall, hugging a pillow to her chest. She nodded, urging him on.

"Ted panicked," Eric said. "Without John's money, he couldn't keep the business going. He shot John, killing him. Then he drove the body to Rhinelander, Wisconsin, and buried him. In fact, that's where I am right now. I notified the police, and they dug up the body today."

There was a long pause on the line, the silence stretching unbearably. Eric's heart pounded in his chest. Finally, Kevin spoke.

"My God, that is amazing," he said. "Dennis, what are you thinking?"

"Crikey!" Dennis said, his voice alive with excitement. "That is an incredible story."

Eric blinked, caught off guard by their reactions. "You're not concerned about having a murderer driving a FeeGo-sponsored race car?" he asked.

"Of course not," Dennis said, his laugh warm and reassuring. "You didn't kill anyone, Eric. Hell, you weren't even alive when the murder took place. This is an incredible story, and if I'm being honest, I'm thrilled to have FeeGo involved. Subscriptions are going to go through the roof."

Eric let out a long breath, relief washing over him. "Thank you, Dennis. I can't tell you how much that means to me." He glanced at Carly, who was smiling broadly, and gave her a wink.

"While I have you on the phone, let me run an idea by you," he said. "My girlfriend, Carly—Dr. Carly Pellegrino—who wrote the article you're familiar with, recently signed a book deal to tell the story I just told you. I was wondering if FeeGo would be interested in buying the film rights to the book. I think it would make an awesome movie or documentary."

Carly sat up straighter, her eyes wide with surprise.

"Hell yes," Dennis said without hesitation. "We would definitely be interested. Have her agent call me directly."

Eric grinned, feeling a surge of satisfaction. "Fantastic. I'll make sure that happens."

After a few more pleasantries, the call ended. Carly was still staring at him, her mouth slightly open in disbelief.

"You're crazy," she said, laughing.

"Looks like you're going to need an agent."

CHAPTER 45

The room was cloaked in the stillness of early morning when Eric stirred awake. The faint glow of the clock on the nightstand read 5:07. For a moment, he lay there, listening to Carly's soft, rhythmic breathing, her curls spilled across the pillow. She looked peaceful, and for a brief second, Eric debated staying where he was, curling back into the warmth of her presence. But his mind was already elsewhere, tugged by an urgency he couldn't ignore.

Quietly, he slid out of bed and grabbed his clothes, moving with practiced care to avoid waking her. Each step felt amplified in the silence, every tiny sound a whisper of guilt trailing him. He pulled on his coat, pausing for a final glance at Carly, before slipping out the door and into the predawn chill.

The air outside bit at his cheeks, and a fine layer of frost sparkled on the windshield of his car under the dim parking lot lights. He started the engine, its low rumble breaking the quiet, and reached for the ice scraper. The rhythmic scrape of the plastic blade against glass filled the air, leaving him alone with his thoughts. His breath puffed out in clouds as he worked, the cold cutting through his coat and seeping into his bones. By the time he finished, his fingers were numb, and he climbed into the car, rubbing his hands together as he pulled out of the parking lot.

The Walmart down the street was nearly deserted, its amber lights cast a stark glow over the empty parking lot. Inside, the store was eerily quiet, the only sounds the faint buzz of refrigeration units and the occasional squeak of a shopping cart. Eric walked the aisles with purpose, his steps echoing on the linoleum. In the garden section, he found a sturdy shovel, its handle smooth and cool to the touch. He carried it with him to the hardware section, where he selected a flat blade screwdriver and a box cutter.

At the self-checkout, the cashier stationed nearby gave him a cursory glance but said nothing. Eric bagged his items quickly, the sense of anticipation building in his chest. He returned to the car, stowing the tools carefully in the trunk before driving toward the cabin.

The road stretched ahead of him, bordered by dense woods that seemed to hold their breath in the early morning quiet. When he reached the cabin, he paused at the end of the driveway, his hands gripping the wheel. The structure stood dark and silent against the backdrop of trees, its presence both familiar and alien. There were no cars in the driveway. Phil and Amanda must have gone back to Chicago, leaving the place empty. Eric drove up slowly, parking near the cabin and stepping out into the crisp Wisconsin air.

The shovel felt solid in his grip as he approached the site where the police had dug the day before. The disturbed earth was evident, a patch of raw soil amid the frost-covered ground. He stood for a moment, surveying the area, his breath clouding around him. The memories came unbidden—Ted's memories—flooding his mind with startling clarity. He knew this place intimately, knew its secrets, and knew where to dig.

Eric picked a spot closer to the lake, where the morning light began to streak the sky with hues of pink and orange. The frozen ground resisted at first, the shovel's blade skidding off the surface. But with persistence, he broke through, each movement mechanical, deliberate. The first hole yielded nothing but dirt and roots. Undeterred, he moved a few feet over and tried again. His muscles burned and sweat dampened his shirt despite the cold. The rhythm of digging drowned out everything else—the distant calls of birds, the gentle lap of water against the shore.

On the third attempt, his shovel struck something solid with a dull metallic thud. He froze, his breath catching in his throat. Carefully, he cleared the surrounding dirt, revealing a rusted metal box. It was small and nondescript, but its weight felt immense as he pulled it free from the ground. He brushed the dirt from its lid, his hands trembling slightly.

After filling in the hole, Eric carried the box to the car, placing it carefully on the passenger seat. He gathered up the tools and stashed them in the trunk. The drive back into town was a blur, his mind racing with the implications of what he'd found. As he drove, the first hints of sunlight were filtering through the clouds, signaling the start of a new day.

"Where have you been?" Carly was still in bed, her voice groggy. She propped herself up on one elbow, her hair tousled, and her eyes half-lidded with sleep.

Eric stood by the door, smiling. "I got us some coffee."

Her expression softened, and she sat up, reaching for one of the cups. "You're so sweet," she murmured, the warmth of the cup seeming to rouse her further.

Eric set his coffee on the small corner desk, his movements deliberate. From inside his coat, he pulled the metal box, placing it next to his cup with a muted clink. He shrugged off his coat, draping it over a chair.

Carly's gaze shifted to the box, curiosity flickering across her face. "What's that?" she asked.

"It's a gift."

"For whom?" Her smile was tentative but intrigued.

"For you." He pulled a screwdriver from his back pocket and held it up for her to see. "Want to see what's inside?"

Carly nodded, sliding out of bed and padding barefoot to his side. She watched intently as Eric pried at the lid, the metal resisting with a groan before finally yielding. Inside, something wrapped in plastic and duct tape glinted faintly in the morning light.

"What is that?"

Eric used the box cutter to slice through the tape, revealing neatly stacked bundles of cash. The sight of the money silenced them both for a moment.

"If it's all still there," Eric said quietly, "this should be a little over forty-seven thousand dollars. That should keep the Center going for a few months."

Carly's eyes widened, her hand covering her mouth. "Is that… Driggins' money?"

"It is," Eric said. "When I was Ted and I got up to Rhinelander, I decided not to spend the money. I was afraid it could be traced back to Driggins, so I buried it."

Carly took a step back, sinking onto the edge of the bed. "Oh my God, Eric. I can't take that money."

"Why not?" He shrugged.

She shook her head, her hands trembling slightly. "I'm not sure," she said. "It just feels… wrong."

Eric knelt in front of her, his expression earnest. "What else do you think should happen to it?" he asked. "Should I give it to the police? They don't need it. They know there was a murder, but the guy who committed it is dead. It has no value as evidence."

When she didn't respond, he continued. "Should I spend it on myself? What good is going to come of that?"

Eric sat beside Carly on the bed and reached for her hand. "A man died several decades ago because of this money. Maybe now it can do some good by helping to keep the center open and do more research into reincarnation."

Carly looked at him, her eyes full of questions. "I thought you weren't sure if you believed in reincarnation."

"I'm not sure," Eric said. "But I believe in you."

Epilogue

Eric turned off the blacktop onto an unmarked side road, the tires crunching against loose gravel. Dust kicked up behind the rented SUV, swirling in the rearview mirror like a ghostly trail. He gripped the wheel firmly, carefully navigating the ruts and potholes that marred the road's uneven surface. On either side, endless pastures of wispy prairie grass rolled gently in the wind, penned in by barbed wire and the occasional decorative split rail fence. The land stretched wide and open, broken only by the jagged silhouette of the Rocky Mountains far in the distance. Their snowcapped peaks seemed to rise from the earth like ancient sentinels, eternal and watchful.

For several minutes, they drove in silence, the only sound the muted rumble of the engine and the occasional rattle of loose items in the car. Although Eric had never set foot here before, a strange familiarity settled over him, like stepping into a half-forgotten dream.

"Do you recognize any of this?" he asked, his voice quieter than usual, as if afraid to disturb the spell of the landscape.

Carly glanced out the window, her eyes scanning the terrain. "Maybe," she said slowly, her tone laced with uncertainty. "I feel like we're getting close to the ranch."

Eric nodded. "I think you're right. Isn't it weird knowing the way to a place we've never been before?"

Carly's excitement grew as they approached. Her hand instinctively rested on the door handle, her body leaning forward slightly, trying to take in as much of the scenery as possible. "I know where we are," she said suddenly, her voice tinged with wonder. "The house should be up here on the left."

Eric smiled at her enthusiasm. She had been the one to track down the address, combing through old maps and property records to confirm his memories. The former Bennett Ranch was now the Fillmore-Beaumont Ranch, and Carly had called ahead, speaking to Deidre Fillmore, who had read Carly's book and eagerly invited them to visit.

Sure enough, a large wooden sign came into view, its weathered letters reading, "Fillmore-Beaumont Cattle Company." The driveway wound its way toward a sprawling, modern home, flanked by several large outbuildings. The house stood in stark contrast to the rustic surroundings, its clean lines and contemporary design a far cry from the rugged simplicity Eric had envisioned.

Despite its grandeur, something about the ranch felt empty. The horse corral near one of the barns held only a few disinterested horses, their tails swishing lazily at flies. Several vehicles were parked in the driveway, but no one was in sight. The quiet felt unnerving, as if the place was holding its breath.

Eric pulled the car to a stop in front of the house and turned off the engine. He sat for a moment, his hands resting on the wheel, staring at the modern house, his mind a jumble, but eager to learn whatever secrets the ranch had to offer. "That certainly isn't EJ's house," he said finally.

"No," Carly agreed. "It's too new."

They sat in silence, the gravity of the moment settling over them like a heavy load. Finally, Eric broke the quiet. "Are you ready for this?"

Carly hesitated, then nodded. "I think so."

They stepped out of the car and approached the front door, the sound of their footsteps muted by grass and dirt. Eric pressed the doorbell and stepped back, standing close enough to Carly that their shoulders brushed. The faint ring of the chime echoed from within, followed by the sound of footsteps.

The door opened to reveal a woman with auburn hair pulled back in a ponytail, her cheeks flushed as if she'd been hard at work. She held a dishtowel in one hand and smiled warmly at them. "Dr. Pellegrino?"

Carly extended her hand. "Please, call me Carly. And this is Eric."

Eric offered his hand as well. "It's nice to meet you."

"I'm Deidre. Please, come in." She opened the door wider and stepped aside.

The house was impeccably maintained, its interior a blend of rustic charm and modern luxury. Deidre led them through the home to the kitchen, where the smell of coffee, bacon, and freshly baked bread lingered in the air. The countertops gleamed under the soft glow of pendant lights, and a copy of Carly's book sat prominently on the counter.

"I was just cleaning up from breakfast," Deidre said, gesturing to the sink. "My husband, the kids, and all the hands left early this morning to round up cattle from the summer pastures. They'll be gone most of the day."

"I hope we're not interrupting you," Carly said.

"Oh, goodness no," Deidre replied with a laugh. "I appreciate the distraction."

Eric's eyes lingered on the book, its spine creased from eager reading. The realization that Carly's work had become a bestseller still filled him with pride. He thought about the documentary Dennis was producing, the way Carly's research was reaching audiences far beyond what either of them had imagined.

Deidre noticed his gaze and smiled. "I'd like both of you to sign that before you leave," she said.

"We'd be happy to," Carly assured her.

"I was shocked when I realized our ranch was the one in your book," Deidre continued. "When I told my husband, he was just as surprised."

"How long have you lived here?" Carly asked.

"Thirteen years," Deidre replied. "But my parents bought the ranch in 1976. I grew up in a house just up the road. This house was built in

1998. My mom passed away not long after they moved in, and my dad passed in 2012. After that, my husband, kids, and I moved in."

"Do you know if the original house was still here when your parents bought the property?" Carly asked.

"No, the original house burned down before I was born," Deidre said. "My parents bought the place for the land and eventually built a new house where the old one once stood. There's an old cabin still standing out near the woods, though. It's in rough shape, but it's out there. Do you think that could be the cabin from your book?"

"It could be," Carly said, smiling. "Is it okay if we go see it?"

"Oh, sure," Deidre said, wiping her hands on the towel. "I have to finish up here, but you're welcome to take a look. I'll give you directions."

Deidre walked them to the front door, pointing out the path to the old cabin. "Don't forget to sign my book when you come back," she added with a grin.

They climbed back into the SUV and followed the dirt path through sprawling pastures. The sun climbed higher in the sky, casting a golden light over the landscape. Three times, Eric had to stop the car to open and close gates, the metal latches cold and rough against his hands.

As they crested a small hill, the cabin came into view. It sat alone amid the tall grass, a crumbling relic of a bygone era. The weathered logs were gray and splintered, the roof sagging inward. One side wall had collapsed completely, leaving the interior exposed to the elements. And yet, despite its ruin, the cabin exuded a quiet dignity, a testament to the lives it had once sheltered.

"This is it," Eric said softly, pulling the car to a stop near the front porch.

Carly stared at the cabin, her breath catching. "Yes, it is," she whispered.

They stepped out of the car and approached the structure slowly, as if afraid to disturb the memories embedded in the wood. Eric tested the steps, their creaks echoing in the still air. "Be careful," he said, offering Carly his hand.

She climbed the steps cautiously, joining him on the porch. Together, they looked out over the valley, where the distant Rockies stood framed by a vivid blue sky.

"It's a beautiful view," Carly said.

"I remember sitting out here with you at the end of the day, watching the sun set over the mountains or tracking a thunderstorm as it moved across the valley," he said, his voice filled with nostalgia. "I think it was the happiest time of any of my lives, being here with you."

"And now we're here again."

"Yes, we are." Eric thought for a moment. "I might have lied. Maybe the happiest time of all my lives has been these past several months. I've loved sharing time with you."

"I've been happy too," Carly said, her eyes shining.

Eric reached into his pocket and pulled out a small velvet box. Opening it, he revealed a delicate ring. "Why don't we make it permanent?" he asked. "Carly, will you do me the honor of becoming my wife?"

Carly gasped, her hand covering her mouth. Tears filled her eyes as she whispered, "Oh my God. Yes, I'll be your wife." She threw her arms around his neck and gave him a long kiss

Eric chuckled, his own voice cracking with emotion. "I think I'm supposed to put this ring on your finger before we kiss."

Carly laughed, pulling back just enough to offer her left hand.

Eric placed the ring on her finger. "Now you can kiss me."

And she did.

Acknowledgments

At times, the writing process can be a lonely endeavor, sitting alone in front of a blank screen. At other times, creating a book can be very collaborative, involving several people, all of whom deserve recognition and appreciation for their contribution to the overall effort.

Let me start by thanking my children, Shelby and Louis. Often, without meaning to, they provide me with inspiration that gets me through those tough days when my mind is jumbled and the words won't come. Thank you both for your love and support. I am blessed to be your father.

I'd also like to thank my friend Connie Smith. Throughout the writing of my previous novel, *A Thousand Ways Home*, as well as this book, Connie was fighting cancer. Even so, she constantly encouraged and inspired me, both through her words and the tenacious way she fought her illness. Sadly, Connie did not live long enough to see the finished version of this novel, but her support and encouragement helped get it over the finish line. Thank you, Connie.

A special thanks to my friend and editor, Sean Ironman. Despite not liking this book (it's an inside joke), he helped to make it much better than I could have on my own. Whenever I fall off the trail and get lost, I can count on Sean to bring me back. Thank you for all your help, Sean.

Finally, I am fortunate to have Amy Zizich Beyer in my corner proofreading the final manuscript. For this novel, she went above and beyond to complete her task, even after her laptop stopped working. Thank you for going the extra mile, Amy. I appreciate your help and your friendship.

About the Author

Lou Mindar is the author of *A Thousand Ways Home, The Ones That Got Away, Driven,* and the novella collection, *Road Stories.* He is a graduate of Western Illinois University and received his MFA in creative writing from the University of Central Florida. He lives in Wisconsin.

Other Books by Lou Mindar

Road Stories

Promised Land (Novella)

Driven

The Ones That Got Away

A Thousand Ways Home